Dawn,
Enjoy +

☺ y
Tamara

MW00676112

Promises Made,
Promises Kept

© 2007 Tamara Angela Grant.

All rights reserved. Printed in the U.S. A.

No part of this publication may be reproduced
or transmitted in any form or by any means,
electronic or mechanical, including photocopy,
recording or any information storage and retrieval
system now known or to be invented, without the
permission in writing from the author, except by a
reviewer who wishes to quote brief passages in
connection with a review written for inclusion in a
magazine, newspaper or broadcast.

Published in the United States by
Beckham Publications Group, Inc.

ISBN: 0-931761-33-6
10 9 8 7 6 5 4 3 2 1

Library of Congress Control Number: 2007923097

Promises Made, Promises Kept

Tamara Angela Grant

THE Beckham
PUBLICATIONS GROUP, INC.
Silver Spring

Prologue

"YEAH MAN, I'M ABOUT TO DROP HER OFF RIGHT NOW. I'LL HIT YOU BACK in a few."

Mark made the turn into my apartment complex. Two right turns and a left around the circle. He pulled up and parked in front of building 2510.

"Girl, you pissy drunk! Can you make it up the steps?"

"I'm aight! I been way-mo drunk than this!"

I wasn't lying. I had gotten fucked-up way worse than this before. I was still coherent enough to push Mark's hand off of my thigh as it crept up my leg.

"Oh, so it's like that, Lil' Mama?"

"Hell, yeah! I'm out." Truth was I could have used a little help getting out of the car. As the cool evening air hit me, I felt a second wind. Hopefully it would be enough to get to me to my apartment.

I stumbled out of the car. Mark laughed.

"F - Fuck you Mark!" I stuttered, as I slammed the passenger door to his black on black Benz CLK 500.

"Whatever. Later Mia," he said as he drove off.

As I walked to the door, I remember thinking that it was awfully quiet out for an early Saturday morning. The people in the building next door were usually outside drinking beers and playing music to usher in the weekend.

I tripped again and decided that the high heels had to come off. Fumbling through my purse, I pulled out my keys. I reached my front door, high heels in hand, and never was I so happy that I lived on the bottom floor. It took me a second to get the key in the keyhole. My vision was a bit doubled and I made a mental note to lay off the Long Island iced tea the next time I went out.

The lock clicked and I was home sweet home. Breathing a sigh of relief, all I could think of was getting in the bed and sleeping off the intoxication.

I didn't even bother to turn on any lights. I couldn't take anything that would make my head pound any worse.

I thought for a second where my girl Carmen could be at this time of night. Then I remembered that she told me that she would be staying the night over at her boyfriend Manny's house.

Great. I couldn't take another night of her and Manny's sexcapades. There was only so much, "Aye Papi" that a girl could take.

As I entered my bedroom, I let the heels and purse land where they may. The street lamp from outside cast an eerie shadow in the room.

The next thing I remember was an arm coming from behind, grabbing me around my throat. The arm squeezed relentlessly as I clawed, trying to be released. I was picked up off of my feet and thrown to the bed. *What the fuck was happening?*

"What the hell do you want?" I screamed.

The answer was a back handed slap to my left cheek. I rolled off the bed and scrambled across the room, searching for my heels. At least then I could clock this mutherfucka in the eye or something.

He pounced on me as I hit the floor. He was dressed in all black: black gloves, black mask, black hoodie, black sweat pants, black tennis shoes.

We struggled on the floor for what seemed like hours. He was obviously stronger than me, but I wasn't about to lie down and die. Not tonight.

It surprised me that I gave up such a fight considering how drunk I was. I guess my adrenaline was pumping something fierce. He finally punched me hard enough that it stunned me for a sec. As I lay there, I felt cloth inserted into my mouth and knew that he was gagging me. Shit! Had I even screamed for help this whole time? Did my neighbor next door, Ms. Lee, hear the commotion?

He grabbed me again, this time throwing me on the bed. He tied my hands and legs to the bedposts. He then straddled me and all I could do at that point was say a silent prayer. That was the only way that I would make it out of this alive.

I saw him pull something out of his pocket. He unwrapped a condom, slid it on. A sharp pain consumed my body as he rammed himself into me. Again and again, he roughly plunged in and out of me. A small cry escaped my lips. I knew that no one heard. He just kept going, as I lay there unable to defend myself. I could not figure out why this was happening. The only thing that I could do as the pain from my vagina burned was transport myself to some far off place. The places that I watched on the Travel Channel flashed through my mind. White sand beaches; azure, blue waters.

Just as I was on the beach, eating a vanilla ice cream cone, he stopped. I lay and waited for what he would do next. He laughed and smacked me again. My body ached all over and my womanly area throbbed from the beating I took. All I could think of was would I ever be able to have children. I was too young for my life to end like this. I tried not to show any fear. Something I learned on the streets. People like him fed off your fear. All I wanted was for this to be over and for me to be alive at the end. I prayed that someone would come to my rescue.

Then he pulled up his pants and got off the bed. He got close to me, up in my face and I could smell his sweat mixed with my scent on him. I prayed that he would leave.

"Bitch, you lucky I don't kill you! I came to bring you a message. Big Deuce say he ain't finished wit you yet! Believe that, 'ho'!"

Shit! I thought all of that was over. And to be honest, I wasn't sure how Big Deuce had become my problem.

Next thing I knew, I passed out after his black, gloved fist connected with my face.

Chapter 1

1993

THE LAST OF THE GUESTS FROM ONE OF MY PARENTS' INFAMOUS PARTIES left at four in the morning. I tried to stay up and be a part of everything, but of course being too young, I was sent to bed. Their parties were always off the chain: plenty of people, music, alcohol, marijuana, amongst other things, and spades games that made people come to blows. I couldn't wait until I was old enough to attend their parties.

I heard the front door close and rolled over in my bed to try and go back to sleep. That's when it began.

"Cliff, what the fuck is up wit' you and Carol?"

Carol was one of my parent's classmates. My parents had just graduated from law school at Georgia State. The plan was for the two of them to become successful attorneys. At seven years old, many of my friends were jealous of me because my parents were still together and they were trying to make a better life for us. Most of my friends came from single parent homes. Not that being from a single parent home was a problem. Hell, when the fighting began in my house, I wished that I was too.

"Here we go again, Patrice! There is nothing going on between Carol and me. I could really get tired of you imagining things!"

"Imagining things! I saw her follow you when you went to get a drink from the kitchen! Just admit that you two are fucking!"

"Hell, no! There's nothing going on between us, Patrice! It's early in the morning and I'm not playing these games with you."

I heard my mother storm off to the kitchen. She was most likely drunk and high. My dad had recently stopped his recreational smoking and drinking in preparation for his career as a lawyer. My mother, on the other hand, still indulged.

Clifton Lawson and Patrice Reed had been an item since they attended Atlanta's Douglas High School. My mother was pregnant with me when she walked across the stage at their graduation. They talked about marriage, but put off their plans until they graduated from college. My dad figured that it would be hard enough to raise a child and study, so he convinced my mother that they should wait. So they got a place and started their life together. After I was born they each took a year off before applying to the university. They worked as they attended community college. The next year, they each applied and were accepted at Georgia State University and studied law.

I heard them fight many times, but I also saw them make up. I just always thought that maybe they were stressed out, because having a kid and going to school had to be tough.

"I won't have you cheating on me, Clifton Lawson!" A dish crashed somewhere in the living room. I visualized my dad ducking as the glass shattered against the wall. I curled up with my pillow in the bed. It would be another rowdy night.

"Patrice, come on! You know I'm not cheating! You're just high. You get real paranoid when you're high."

"I wasn't high when I saw the way that you were staring at her tonight! I bet you want her don't you?" my mother cried out. "I bet you already fucked her!"

"I'm only going to tell you once more! I don't want that woman!"

"Well, then why haven't we made wedding plans, Cliff? What, I'm good enough to play house with and have your child, but not good enough to marry?"

I heard my dad growl angrily. "You know that's not true Patrice! I don't know what world you're living in, but you know that's not true."

Another dish hit the wall. I heard a slap and I knew that was the sound of my mother's open hand connecting with the chocolate brown skin on my dad's cheek. A commotion followed and that meant that she attacked him. I had seen it happen before. I knew that he loved her, but I was also smart enough to know that it was just a matter of time before he was fed up with her abuse.

"Patrice! Get off of me! Stop acting like this!" my dad said between breaths.

"No, you stop Cliff! I'm taking Mia and I'm leaving!"

"You can't do that, Patrice. You can't take my baby girl from me. Especially when I haven't done anything."

"Yes, I can!"

I heard my mother breathing heavily as she walked toward my bedroom. A sliver of light from the hallway entered my room as she opened the door. I closed my eyes tightly and pretended to be sleeping.

"Mia! Mia! Get up!" she whispered loudly.

I could hear my father yelling from the hallway for her to leave me alone and saying that she could not drive while she was under the influence.

I continued to fake being asleep. I didn't want any part of this. I hated when they went at each other. Their relationship was always one of two extremes; either they were in love or they hated each other.

My mother grabbed my jacket and wrapped it around me as she picked me up. I groggily wrapped my arms around my shoulder, making sure to keep my eyes closed.

She walked into the hallway and grabbed her keys and purse.

"Patrice, don't do this! Just calm down. We can talk about this."

"There is nothing to talk about Cliff. I know what I saw." She pushed his arm off of her shoulder. I opened my eyes slightly and saw the distress on my dad's face. There was a pile of broken dishes in the corner adding to the leftover remnants of the party.

My eyes met my dad's. The heartbreaking expression on his face let me know that my mother was having another one of her episodes. I wondered why she had to act like that. My dad was a good man. I knew that we were on our way over to Aunt Lena's, my mother's twin and best friend.

My dad mouthed the words 'I love you, Mia' to me as my mother carried me out of the door. I knew somewhere deep down that this night was different from all the rest when they fought. My dad stood in the doorway, conflicted over how he would continue to live his life like this. I, myself, wasn't sure how he could take it anymore. I knew that from that night on, things in our home had changed forever.

Chapter 2

I FAKED LIKE I WAS ASLEEP THE ENTIRE DRIVE TO MY AUNT LENA'S HOUSE.
She lived across town in Stone Mountain. It took us thirty minutes
more than it should have for us to get there because my mother
was high as a kite. She drove the speed limit so that she wouldn't
get pulled over by the police.

I knew that it was the butt crack of dawn when we got there
and it didn't matter to my aunt one bit. That was the cool thing
about the relationship between my mom and Aunt Lena.

They were identical twins. Aunt Lena always said that I made
them triplets because we all shared the same caramel skin, long
brown hair, and slanted hazel eyes.

When we came in, the smell of coffee greeted us at the door.
My mom took me to my cousin Mookie's room. His real name was
Michael, but I can't remember anyone ever calling him by anything
other than his nickname. Being only a year older than me, our
moms raised us more like siblings than cousins.

My mom took my jacket off as I continued to fake my sleep,
and put me in the bed beside Mookie, tucking us in tightly. She
left the door cracked and went back to the dining room with Aunt
Lena.

"Mimi, what's up now? Aunt Tricie actin' a fool again?" he asked,
rolling over. I knew he wasn't asleep.

"Yeah, she flipped out on my dad."

"Dang. Uncle Cliff is a good dude. At least you have a dad.
Mine is dead."

We sat in silence for a second. Mookie never said anything to his mom, but I knew that never meeting his dad would always haunt him. His dad was a big time dope dealer on the Westside from Bankhead. Aunt Lena was living large with him, with all of the jewelry, cars, and more cash than she could spend. When she was at the hospital in labor with Mookie, his dad was killed in a drive-by on the way to the hospital and so they never got a chance to meet one another.

One of his business partners gave Aunt Lena all of his dad's money from his safe and helped her to by a house in Stone Mountain, to get away from that life. She was smart enough to put the rest of the money away in savings. She worked a part-time job as a nurse at the hospital and the rest of the time, she spent taking care of Mookie. She vowed that she would raise him so that he would never end up like his father.

We sat and listened to our moms talk. My mom broke down in tears as she talked about her accusation of my dad's infidelity.

"But Tricie, did you really see anything happen between them? You know that you get paranoid sometimes."

"I know what I saw! That bastard wants to get with Carol! That's why we haven't gotten married yet."

"Tricie, have you taken your medication lately?"

Mookie and I looked at each other. We snuck out of the bed and inched closer to the cracked door to listen in on their conversation.

"Fuck that medication! I don't need to be all drugged up on that shit!"

"But Tricie, you know what the doctor said. You need it so that you can think clearly. You weren't like this when you were on your medication," Aunt Lena said in her familiar soothing tone.

Medication? Hell, Aunt Lena made it sound like my mother was a nut case or something. The only thing that I had ever seen my mother medicate herself with was alcohol and weed.

"Humph!" my mother said completely disregarding what my aunt asked her. "Anyway, me and Mia are going to stay the night until I can get my head clear. I can't face Cliff right now."

"You know my home is your home. I just hope that you think about this. You can't keep treating Cliff like you are. He is a good man, and I'm sure he doesn't want to keep putting up with you and your mood swings. You need to make sure that you get some help, Tricie. Think about Mimi too. She needs her dad and Cliff loves that girl to death."

My mom took another sip of her coffee and rubbed her hands against her temples. She always looked like she was in a constant struggle with herself. I knew that she didn't want to leave my dad, but it was like she was another person when she flew into a rage.

When we went back home the next day, the house was cleaned up. Daddy's car was gone. I figured we would see him after he came home from church. My mother took a long nap and I sat up and watched some of the Sunday morning television shows while I ate a bowl of cereal. Mom got up around noon and moped around the house the rest of the day. The time ticked by and my dad still hadn't come home or even called to say where he was. I went outside to play with a few of my friends from the neighborhood. When the streetlights came on and my dad still hadn't come home, I knew that there was a problem.

"Mama, where's Daddy?" I asked, as we ate dinner.

"Mia, he left us. He's not coming back."

The words hit me like the anvil dropped by the Road Runner on Wile E. Coyote; predicted, but still unexpected. I shifted my peas around my plate. My mother got up from the table and put her plate in the sink.

"I don't understand Mama. Why would he do that? You guys fight all of the time and he's never left before."

"Yeah well, he doesn't want to marry me. So he's gone Mia." Her tone was dry and her facial expression didn't show any feeling.

"Where is he? Is he at Grandma's? I could call him and tell him to come home," I said as I got up to run for the phone.

"Stop it, Mia!" she screamed. The pitch in her voice was enough to stop me in my tracks. "He doesn't love us! *He is not coming back!*"

I refused to believe her. My dad would never do that.

"Mama, you're lying! My daddy wouldn't leave us!"

She grabbed me by my arms and shook me. We were both crying. It was the first time that I felt hatred for my mother.

"He's gone Mia! He said that it wasn't working between us."

"But what about me? Why would you make him leave, Mama? Why can't you act right?"

My mother just stood in the middle of the floor, tears flowing.

I would be asking that question for years to come. I was convinced from that point on that my mother had driven him away.

My dad never came back home. The next thing I know, the locks were changed on the front door. He came by a few times and my mother made me sit in silence with her like we were hiding from the Jehovah's Witness, as he banged on the door. She hung up the phone and wouldn't accept his phone calls.

He would come over to Aunt Lena's house when I was there on the weekends that my mom worked. Then she found out that he was coming and she threatened to call the police on him and get a restraining order to keep him away from us. He only came by Aunt Lena's a few more times after that.

I later learned that he continued to pay for the bills at our house while he stayed with my grandmother. His side of the family still called at first, but all contact with them eventually stopped. I saw them sometimes on the holidays, but that stopped too. It was hard because we would always spend time with all of our family. I figured that they took sides with my dad, but that left me caught out there. I could never figure out why my grandmother and my aunts and uncle stopped coming by to see me, or even calling as much, for that matter.

Things changed very drastically. I know that my grandmother was never too fond of them being together anyway, but I thought that at least she and I had a better relationship than that. I guess she got tired of dealing with my mother and her rage. But she still could have been there for me though.

I was then confined to the prison of being with my mother and her fluctuating moods. The only relief that I had was the time that

I spent at Aunt Lena's. The rest of the time, I spent trying to figure out how my dad could just up and leave like that. I mean, fine, he and my mom couldn't get along, but how do you just up and leave your child? I wanted him to fight for me. But I quickly learned that everyone couldn't live up to your expectations.

The last time that I saw him, I was at my Aunt Lena's for the weekend. Mookie and I were in his room listening to the Outkast ATLiens CD. Mookie was like most young African-American boys at that time; he wanted to get into the music business.

I heard the knock at the front door. My aunt answered the door and I saw my dad standing there looking raggedy. It looked like he hadn't had a good meal, any sleep, or changed his clothes in a few days.

"Hey Lena, can you give this to Mia please?"

I stood at the bedroom door and watched as my dad gave her a teddy bear and a small jewelry box.

"Look Cliff, I don't want to be in the middle of this thing with you and Tricie."

"There is no thing with me and Patrice. She needs help. I called and told her that I was willing to be there while she gets the help she needs, and she didn't want to. I can't do this by myself."

"I understand, but you know that she is sick. She's not in her right mind."

"Exactly the reason why she needs help. I have to get myself together so that I can get custody of Mia. There is not much that I can do now because I don't really have the money to take care of her by myself right now the way that I want to. You know that Patrice and I aren't married so she has all of the legal rights to Mia. I want to go about this when I'm fully prepared. Please watch out for my princess for me."

"Is that your dad, Mimi?" Mookie asked.

"Yeah," I said as I closed the bedroom door. I couldn't believe that he would be that pitiful. If he was a real man, he would have taken me with him right then and not been such a coward, leaving me behind.

"Why don't you go say something to him?"

"Forget him. He left me. I don't want to be bothered with him anymore."

"Come on, Mimi. You love your dad."

I just leaned against the dresser with my arms crossed. I loved my dad, true, but by now it had been almost three years since he left. I didn't feel like he made enough effort to fight for me, or his relationship with my mom for that matter. I mean, I could understand that they weren't going to be together, but what about me?

"Whatever."

Mookie went back to listening to the music as he turned on the Play Station. He handed me a controller and set up the game. I went and took one last glance out of the bedroom door as my dad walked away. It would be another six years before I saw him again.

Chapter 3

2002

"I'll be there in a minute, Marissa."

"Well, hurry up, my brother is waiting."

I hung up the phone and turned to take one last look in the mirror. I looked too cute in a pink Baby Phat sweat suit and pink Timberland boots to match. I smoothed my hair back into a ponytail, threw my pink lip gloss in my purse, grabbed my overnight bag, and threw my skates over my shoulder. My sixteenth birthday was right around the corner, but I had to admit that the curves on my body said that I was older than the sixteen years old that was around the corner.

My girlfriend Marissa was going with me to my Aunt Lena's. We were tired of the scene in the SWATS, so we were going to go skating on the Eastside at Golden Glide. Marissa's fine ass older brother Brian was dropping us off at the East Point MARTA station so we could ride the train to Indian Creek where Mookie would pick us up.

I locked my bedroom door and walked toward the living room. My mom sat next to her latest victim on the couch. The new Juvenile CD played on the stereo as they laughed and giggled with one another.

"Hey Mimi! This is-," she paused. Damn, she didn't even know his name. I'm glad I got the lock put on my door. I couldn't trust my mother not to bring junkies into the house. Then and again, she was becoming a junkie herself.

"Keith, baby. I'm Keith," he said extending his hand to me. He was as crazy as he looked if he thought I was down for cordial intros.

"Yeah, whatever," I said, as I looked him up and down. Meanwhile, my mother leaned back against the couch and threw her leg over his. She took her toes and massaged his crotch as she took another swallow of vodka. That's the other thing that my mother has been doing. She's become a serious freak. At least two to three different men a week. And that accounted for the ones that I saw.

I felt my stomach lurching as she continued with the PDA, so I took that as my opportunity to get the hell on.

"Where are you going, young lady?"

What the hell? She hadn't been concerned about where I was going for the past few years. No need to get her crazy ass started up though. I had plans tonight.

"Marissa's brother is taking us to the train station so we can go to Aunt Lena's, remember?" What kind of question was that to ask her? Hell no, she didn't remember.

She just shrugged and turned her attention back to Keith. "Have fun sweetie. And don't do anything that I wouldn't do."

What the fuck! I wasn't sure what the limit on that was. I sighed as I walked out of the door. I couldn't stand to look at my mother lately. With all of the drinking and smoking she did, I wasn't sure how she kept her job as a legal secretary. Hell, she was probably sleeping with the senior partner at the firm to solve that problem.

I got to Marissa's house and rang the bell. Her brother Brian answered the door.

Did I tell you that Brian Walters was fine as shit? He was 19 years old, 6'2" with a stocky build, broad shoulders, and his bow legged stance drove me crazy. He had this rich, dark chocolate skin and when he smiled, he flashed perfect white teeth. I was still a virgin and wouldn't mind giving all of that up for him. He was also a dope dealer, so I knew off the top he was bad news. But I didn't care. When I saw him, I got this tingling in my stomach, amongst other places.

"Is Marissa ready?" I asked as I stepped inside the screen door to the living room.

"No, she's on the phone with some lame. You know my sister like them lames."

Oh God, I think I'm going to pass out. The bass in his voice made me want to do things to him. Nasty things.

"Well, I'll go get her," I said trying to fight the feeling.

He grabbed my arm. "Why don't you wait for her right here? She'll be out in a minute."

We stood in the living room. He pulled me close to him and released the skates and my bags from my grasp. I looked up at him and saw this lustful look in his eye.

"You know Mia, me and you could do things." He licked his full lips and the moistness of them made me want to taste them.

What! Me and Brian doing things?

"Like what?" I asked, trying to be cool. Actually, my heart was beating so fast I thought that if I spoke again, it would beat right out of my mouth.

"You know," he said, as he grinded against me. I felt him poking me. "Mia, you a grown woman now. Look at these curves you got." He ran his hand down my spine and stopped as he held my behind in the palm of his hands. Brian leaned in and kissed me on my neck. A river started running between my legs. I wanted this dude and one day I would do something about it. He lifted my face to his and softly planted his lips on mine. Our tongues danced together and I suddenly realized that we were kissing. I swear, if Marissa didn't come out of that room, I would be undressed in the middle of this living room in two seconds flat.

Brian stepped back and looked at me. I took in a deep breath.

"So what's up with me and you, Mia?"

"I—I don't know. I didn't know there *was* a me and you."

Just then Marissa came out from her room. "Mia, I didn't know you were here."

"Yeah girl, just kicking it with Brian" I answered. Marissa better be happy that she came out when she did or else her brother and me would have been going half on a baby. I picked up my bags and my charm bracelet jingled. The bracelet was the last gift that I had gotten from my dad. The gift that he brought over with the teddy bear and a note promising that he loved me and would be back for me.

"Ya'll ready?" Marissa asked.

"Yeah," I said, eyeing Brian. I knew messing with him was not good for me. But it was so tempting.

During the entire ride to the train station, he kept looking at me in the backseat from the rearview mirror. I knew I had to leave that alone. Among other things, he was my girl's brother. That couldn't be a good situation.

I got out of the car and tried my best to ignore him.

"Later, Marissa. Later Mia," he said as we grabbed our things. My name coming from his lips almost made me melt. When Marissa wasn't looking, he licked his lips at me. I bit my lip and pretended not to see his gesture.

Mookie picked us up at the Indian Creek station. We had a good time at Golden Glide and we decided to go to the Waffle House afterwards. It was Marissa's first time coming with me to Aunt Lena's house.

Marissa was my girl but she could be a ghetto snob sometimes. I was surprised that she was so cool tonight. I couldn't fault her for her attitude thought. She came by it honestly. Her mother was a ghetto snob too. She was the type to put clothes on her back before she paid a bill and to act like her daughter wasn't the 'ho' she was and her son wasn't supplying dope to all the fiends in Southwest Atlanta.

When we got back to the house, Aunt Lena was gone. Being a nurse, she worked from seven at night until seven in the morning, Mookie and me were usually there alone when I spent the night.

I made up the beds in the guest room for Marissa and me. We eventually fell asleep after she talked my head off about Jason, her stupid boyfriend that always cheated on her. I couldn't figure out why she even liked him. He was a lame just as Brian said.

I got up in the middle of the night to get something to drink. I had a craving for some warm milk and cookies. Mookie and I had a ritual of sharing midnight snacks so I went to his room to see if he was down.

That's when I heard noises, heavy breathing, and the bed squeaking. When I got closer to the room, I heard Marissa yell out in pleasure. I peeked in through the cracked door and saw her riding my cousin like a bucking bronco. *That heifer*! She came with me as a guest and she had the nerve to sneak and fuck my cousin. And Mookie. I wouldn't bring anymore of my girlfriends around him, that's for damn sure! I'm not a hater, but damn!

I quickly grabbed my snack and went back to my room. I was disgusted. They didn't even know that I was awake and knew what they were doing. As I raised my glass of milk, my bracelet jingled and I thought of my dad. He gave me the bracelet as a promise that he would be back for me. That was six years ago and I hadn't seen or heard from him.

Then my mind switched to Brian. I wondered if he could make me scream like Mookie made Marissa scream. Marissa got around, to say the least, and she asked me all the time what I was waiting on. I always thought that I would wait on my knight in shining armor: the guy who would come and sweep me up off my feet. The more I thought about it, I don't think that he has directions to the hood. If Marissa could fuck my cousin, I was going to get mine from her brother. Why not? I had fantasized about him for so long.

I jingled the bracelet and played with the charms. Sorry, Daddy. I thought about the years that I waited on him to come back and love me. It was time to start looking for love somewhere else.

Chapter 4

I WOKE UP ON APRIL 13, 2002, SMILING. IT WAS MY SWEET SIXTEEN. I decided to play sick and stay home from school. Once again, I had plans. When I unlocked my bedroom door, I put on an act of coughing and sniffles that deserved an Emmy Award. My mother brushed past me in the hallway already dressed for work.

"You don't have to play me, Mimi. Stay home for your birthday," she smiled slyly. I had to laugh. Who was I to try to fool her? She knew all of the tricks of the trade.

"Thanks Mama." I reached out and gave her a hug. She returned the gesture. For that moment, it felt good to be in my mother's embrace. I inhaled her perfume and it took me back to a familiar place a time when I felt secure in my parents' love. She hugged me a little tighter and gave me a kiss on the cheek.

"Happy Birthday, Lady."

"Thanks, Mama," I smiled.

"You should go in my room and check it out. There may be something in there for you." She winked at me and grabbed her car keys and she was out the door.

A large pink box was on the bed with a note addressed to me. I opened it to find a gift certificate to Rich's and a Coach bag that I wanted. I read the note.

> Dear Mimi,
>
> I know that I haven't been the best mother lately. It's just that it's been so hard to deal with everything. Please know that I love you more than I love myself. I really don't mean to hurt you like I do. I'm struggling emotionally more than you'll

ever know. *A piece of me died when your dad left. I have been
so consumed with my own pain, that I haven't spent much
time worried about yours. Please know that things will work
out for you and me. They have to. You and your Aunt Lena
and Mookie are all that I have. The gift certificate is for you to
treat yourself and I know you have wanted a Coach bag forever.
I love you Mimi. You're my everything.*
  Hugs and Kisses,
  Mommy

By the time I finished the letter, I was in tears. It was just
refreshing to know that through everything, my mother loved me.
I always knew that she did, but these past few years were hell.

I got myself some breakfast and called Marissa to tell her to get
my class work for me because I wouldn't be in school today. She
agreed and wished me happy birthday.

I turned up the music and danced around the house to my
Usher 8701 CD. I just hoped that my plans worked out the way
that I wanted them to today.

I showered and dressed and decided to walk outside. Hopefully
I would find who I was looking for. Sure enough, as soon as I
stepped onto my front porch, I saw him riding by in his car. The
car came to a stop in the middle of the street.

"What's happenin' Mia?"

Hopefully me and you. "Nothing."

"You out of school today?" Brian asked.

"Somethin' like that."

"Aight, later." I knew that the stage was set. He would be down
the block to see me in a minute.

I went into the house to dab on a little perfume and put on the
lingerie that I had bought over the weekend. I had never purchased
any before and I decided on a pair of black, lace boy cut underwear
and a lace bustier top. It showed all of the right curves and made my
36 C breasts sit up at attention. If things went the way that I planned,
I would be getting it on with Brian in a few. I put on a tank top and
some jeans over my lingerie so I wouldn't appear too forward.

Within the next ten minutes, Brian was knocking at my door. I conveniently pressed play on the stereo and the CD switched to R. Kelly TP-2.com.

"What a surprise," I said as I opened the door, hand on my hip.

"What's up Mia? You lookin' good," Brian eyed me hungrily.

"Come on in."

Brian came in and stood in the living room. "Your mom's at work?"

"Yeah," I responded.

Now, I could stand here and make small talk or I could go for what I wanted. I wanted Brian. I watched as he bobbed his head to the music.

I closed the door and brushed up against him. His cologne mesmerized me. Brian pulled me in close to him.

"So about the other day? You want to start from there?" he said in reference to the day that he kissed me.

"Why don't you follow me?" I told him taking his hand and leading him to my room. I thought that I would be nervous, but the only thing that I could think of was Brian making me scream out in pleasure the way that I heard Marissa with my cousin. I hoped this was worth it.

Brian followed me into my room. I closed and locked the door. He looked at me strangely.

"I don't want any distractions," I said.

"Yeah, well, me neither. I'm glad that we were on the same page. "

I pushed Brian down on the bed and climbed on top of him. I surprised myself by how forward I was, especially with this being my first time. We started kissing and pulling off each other's clothes. I ran my hands over the ripples of the six-pack of his stomach. He stopped when he got my clothes off and admired the lingerie.

"You wear stuff like this all of the time?"

"Maybe. You should check me out sometimes to see for yourself."

"I should, huh?"

The next thing I knew, Brian had flipped me over and was kissing and licking me all over. He parted my legs, pulled off my panties, and went to work on me with his tongue. I thought that I was going to lose my mind. The way he was going, I thought he would never come up for air. When he did, he took off his boxers and I froze. I refused to believe that he was going to put all of that into me. It had to be physically impossible. He must have seen the look on my face because he let out a small laugh.

"It's cool Mia. I'll be gentle."

I guess that was reassuring. It would have to do, because I wasn't turning back. He slid on the condom and stroked me to make sure that I was wet. I squirmed because his touch made me want to scream all over again.

He slowly entered me. Brian held me close and took his time. When my body finally accepted all of him, he fit like a missing puzzle piece. We began to move to a rhythm all our own. R. Kelly sang about the Greatest Sex and I wondered how he knew what was going through my mind.

I had way too many orgasms to count and I was amazed that a man could make me feel like that. When we were finished, I wanted Brian to stay, but at the same time, I wanted him to go. It was weird because I felt invigorated, like a new woman.

"You okay?" he asked.

"Yeah, I'm good."

"You sure you were a virgin? I mean, your body did things that an experienced woman's body would do."

"I'm sure I *was* a virgin." That was all I could say. I took what he said as a complement but what I really wanted to ask was what was up between us. I didn't want to think that this would be the extent of our relationship.

We lay there entangled with one another until the CD had finished. Brian asked where the bathroom was and went to clean himself up. I just lay there a while longer wondering if he could take me seriously. I had just turned sixteen and there was a three-year age difference between us. Besides, I always saw Brian with these real 'fly-looking' chicks, and although I, myself, was fly too,

I knew that I was younger than he was and he may not want me like that. I could be cool with that if he wouldn't hurt my feelings.

He came back to my room and sat on the edge of the bed. "You sure you okay? I mean, giving away your virginity can be a big thing."

"I'm fine," I said, dismissing all of the thoughts running through my mind. I could tell that he wanted to say something else, but he didn't. Instead he kissed me on the lips.

"I gotta go. I'll catch up with you later, Mia."

I walked him to the door and let him out. He turned around and winked at me. For the next three months, Brian and I snuck around seeing each other. I was sprung off of his sex, but then and again, I had never had anyone else's.

One day I was bored as hell and I decided to go down to Marissa's to see what she was doing. As I strolled down the block, Brian rode past me in his car. I could see a girl seated in the passenger seat. I felt a twinge of betrayal. Since he and I had gotten together, I hadn't seen him with anyone else and that made me feel safe, like he only wanted to be with me. But then I remembered that he wasn't actually my man. He looked at me and waved. I just sighed and kept walking until I reached Marissa's.

I was glad that his car wasn't there when I arrived. Marissa and I decided to hang out on the front porch. Then I saw Brian's car turn back around the corner. I was praying that hoochie wasn't still in the car with him.

He pulled up at the curb and both the driver side and the passenger doors opened. This hood rat looking chick got out. She had on too much makeup, too much gold jewelry, a tank top, and her shorts were all the way up her ass. She was obviously the fast type that didn't really have any respect for herself. When they got out of the car, she ran over to Brian and territorially threw her arms around his neck. He caught my stare and gently pushed Hoochie Mama's arms from around him.

"Chill out, Loqueshia," he said calmly. His eyes never left mine.

Damn. I know I'm a little young, but did he have to flaunt Kelolo, or whatever the 'ho's' name was, in my face? She looked like she got around. She was not cute at all and I couldn't figure out what the hell he was doing with her. Then it hit me. I hoped that he wasn't fucking her and me at the same time. Eeww! I'm glad that we always used protection. I suddenly started to itch just from looking at her.

"But Brian, baby," she whined. Her voice was like nails on a chalkboard.

"Chill out, I said," he repeated. "Why don't you wait for me in the car?"

She sucked her teeth and stomped off toward the car. I rolled my eyes. Marissa laughed. She thought that her brother made interesting choices in women. But this one here was just plain wrong.

"What's up, Mia?" he said as he climbed the porch stairs.

"Whatever," I said throwing up my hand to dismiss him.

Marissa watched the interaction, curiously looking back and forth between us. Brian just stood in front of me waiting for more of a response. I turned and looked the other way ignoring him.

"Oh, so it's like that?" he said.

"I don't know. Why don't you go ask Kelolo over there? She may know what's up." I inched away from him, still looking in the opposite direction.

Brian shook his head and walked into the house.

"What the hell was that?" Marissa asked, eyebrows raised.

"I don't know. That bitch looks stank, don't she?" I said trying to play it off. I knew exactly what Marissa was talking about.

"No hooker! You and Brian - hold up! You fucked my brother didn't you!" she yelled.

I grabbed her and put my hand over her mouth. Muffled words came through my hands.

"Shh! Damn!" I said as I released my hands.

Marissa came up in my face and shook her finger at me. "You 'ho'! You fuckin' around with my brother and I didn't even know it!"

"Sorry, I forgot to mail you your invite, heifer!"

She just stood with her arms crossed and stared at me.

"I know you're not talkin'! This from the chick that met and fucked my cousin the first night they met!" I had to pull her card. She still didn't know I knew.

She burst out laughing. "Dang! You knew about that all this time?"

"Yeah. So I guess we're even."

"Hell, I'm not mad. It's about time, anyway. You were holding on to your virginity like your shit was made of platinum. It's cool, but you could do better than my brother."

"You act like I'm trying to be in a relationship with him or something," I said trying to minimize my feelings for Brian.

"Mia, I know you. Plus, he's your first. I know how that is. You can't play me."

"I'm surprised that you remember your first," I said jokingly.

"Watch it!" she said playfully shoving me.

We laughed as Brian walked out of the house. He paused for a second like he was going to say something. I saw Kelolo peek her head out of the car.

"Look Mia, it's not what you think," he said.

"Brian, you don't know what I think," I said bluntly.

"Brian! Come on!" the hoochie interrupted.

He turned to answer her, but changed his mind.

"I'll call you later, Mia," he said.

"How 'bout, no," I said.

He shook his head and ran down the steps, got in the car and drove off.

Although it felt good to stand up for myself, I couldn't shake the fact that I felt abandoned again. The feeling of betrayal crept up behind me and was starting to smother me.

Marissa sensed that I was hurt. "Girl, there will be others. I told you he's not right for you. There will be someone else."

We sat on the porch and watched as Brian's car turned the corner. I vowed from that point on that I would not let any male get that close to me again. I wouldn't subject myself to the rejection or the hurt again. Fool me once, shame on you. Fool me twice, shame on me.

Chapter 5

I SPENT THE NEXT FEW WEEKS AVOIDING BRIAN. HIS CALLS WERE IGNORED and Marissa hung out at my house more often because she knew the way I felt about how things went down with Brian and me.

She told me over and over again how much he talked about me and how he always asked about me. But I just ignored her and asked that she not relay any more messages for him.

School would be back in session in two weeks so Marissa and I went to the Underground to get our gear together. We had so much fun that day. I hadn't had that much fun in a long time. I needed to just go somewhere that would take my mind off of all of the things that were going on in my life. Marissa and I looked good, as usual. She spent her time flirting with random guys. I wasn't in the mood until Marissa convinced me that I should start getting some numbers from some of the cute guys there.

"Mia, be a teenager for once, why don't you? Meeting guys is what we do. Stop acting all stuck up! Damn!"

I figured, what the hell. It couldn't hurt anything. I came home with about ten numbers, none of which I planned on calling. Okay, maybe I would call the one dude, he was cute and he had some decent conversation.

We walked from the bus stop back to our block. After Marissa went home, I continued up the street.

"Hold up, Mia!"

I knew the voice was Brian's without even turning around to look. I waited for him against my better judgment.

"Why you been avoiding me?" Brian asked as he ran up behind me.

"Let's see, could it be that you bring home these other random hoochies all of the time. Brian, don't act like you don't know that I see it. I don't need that." I couldn't resist unleashing my wrath. He deserved it. I started to walk away.

"Mia," he grabbed my shoulder and turned me around to face him. "I didn't want to hurt you. I really do like you. It just tripped me out a little. You were, like this little girl and all of a sudden, you're this woman. Give me a break! One day you're my little sister's friend and the next we're here at this point," he said, shrugging his shoulders, looking for an ounce of sympathy in my face.

"Yeah, well you didn't have a problem with that when you were sexing' me."

He just stood there for a minute. "Let me walk you the rest of the way to your house."

"No, thank you. I can do it myself. I don't need you!" I meant that in more ways than one.

"Damn it, Mia! Stop pushing me away!" He walked with me anyway. I wasn't about to tell him no again. I wanted him there.

We walked in silence for a minute. "Mia, I don't know what to tell you. I don't want a girlfriend. I'm doing too much right now."

"I don't want to be your girlfriend," I lied. "You could have had the courtesy to consider my feelings before you paraded all of those bitches around me though," I said looking away from him. I know that I had only really seen him with Kelolo, but I knew that there had been others. I couldn't look him in the eye. If I did, it would only bring the tears closer to falling.

"Okay, I can take that. I just don't want you to hate me. I like you, Mia. We just have to give things a little time. I'm out here in these streets. I can't have you waiting around for me and I definitely can't have you in my head all of the time. I need to concentrate to get my grind on."

Yeah, it sounded sincere and maybe that's what I get for choosing him. Brian lifted my chin toward his face.

"We cool?" *Hell, yeah, and more than that.*

"Yeah. I guess."

"Good." He bent down and kissed me. He tasted like strawberries. I didn't give a damn what the flavor was, as long as I could taste him. "Mia, I want you to stay down. You the type of chick that I could get used to callin' my wifey."

I admit, his comment made me go crazy inside, but I would never let it show.

"Look, Brian, I got to go."

"Yeah, just know that I'm not goin' anywhere, Mia."

He kissed me again and I almost fainted. I stepped back and regained my composure as he walked back down the street. My cell phone rang. It was Marissa.

"I saw that. I told you he likes you!"

"Get off my phone, hooker!" I laughed.

"Yeah, well, I just wanted you to know that I saw you two and so did half the block. You need to do better if you trying to keep your shit on the low!"

"Whatever. I'll talk to you later."

We hung up as I opened the front door to the house. The smell of weed and something else that I couldn't place hit me. It was the weekend and my mother was on another binge. I went to my room to hide out.

I turned on the television and dialed my cousin's number. As the phone rang, it beeped signaling that he was on the other line.

"What's up, cuz?" he answered.

"Nothin' much," I said.

"Am I still picking you up tomorrow morning?"

"Please do," I said. Truth was, I would have given anything for him to come and get me now.

"Aight, look, I'm on the other line and it's important, so I'll check you in the morning."

"Later, Mook."

"Later, Mimi."

I threw the phone on my bed as I heard giggling coming from my mother's bedroom. She had company and I wasn't about to listen to all of that tonight. I turned up the volume on the television to drown out her activities. I would be so glad to spend the next two weeks with my aunt and get away from this shit.

I don't know what time I fell asleep, but the banging on the front door made me jump out of my dreams.

"Ms. Lawson! Open up! Fulton County police! Open up!"

I looked at my clock. 2 am. The police? What the hell is going on? They continued banging on the door. I dialed my cousin's number.

"Who dis?" he answered in a groggy voice.

"Mookie, it's Mimi! Stay on the phone with me! I don't know what's going on, but the police are at the door."

I heard him become alert. "What's going on Mimi? What you mean the police? I'm on my way over there!"

"No, just wait a second. Let me see what's going on."

I walked to the living room watching as the red and blue lights flashed against the wall.

"Ms. Lawson, it's the police open up!"

I clutched the phone in my hand as I noticed that the house was silent. Where was my mother? I know all of the banging should have made her wake up. But she was probably passed out from last night.

I cracked the front door and saw two policemen standing on the front porch. I could hear Mookie ask what's going on.

"Hold on, Mook, I'm about to see."

"All right, I ain't going anywhere," he answered. It made me feel a little more secure.

"Mia Lawson?" the black cop asked.

"Yes."

I heard yelling come from the street and then the sound of glass breaking. The white cop ran off of the porch toward the squad car.

"Honey, is anyone else home with you?"

"No," I answered.

"The woman in the back of the patrol car says that she is your mother."

"What?" I asked.

I opened the door a little more to see my mother thrashing around in the back of the cop car. Her legs were hanging out of the shattered back window, blood trickled down one leg.

"Mia! Mia! Get me out of here! Now Mia!" she screamed. My heart raced and I could faintly hear screaming in my ears. Mookie had put my aunt on the phone. Between her screaming and my mother screaming, I was about to go crazy.

"Is that woman your mother?" the officer asked again.

"Yes," I answered sadly.

"Well, if you could get her some clothes, that would be great," he said.

"Clothes? What do you mean?" The officer began to answer when I heard Aunt Lena scream my name again.

"Mia, what the hell is going on over there?"

I suddenly began to cry and I walked down the hallway to get some clothes for my mother as the officer waited at the front doorway. "I don't know, Aunt Lena, please come get me! Hurry please!"

"Honey, me and Mookie left the house as soon as you called. Pack your clothes and let me speak to the officer."

I returned to the living room with an outfit for my mother and I handed the clothes and the phone to the officer. I managed to tell him that it was my aunt and he took the phone. I could hear my mother still calling my name from outside. I couldn't deal with seeing her like that, so I ran to my room to pack. I vaguely heard the officer tell my aunt that my mother was caught breaking into our neighbors' house. She was completely naked and obviously under the influence of drugs and alcohol. Apparently, my neighbor's boyfriend was asleep on the couch and woke up to my mother "performing oral sexual acts on him" as the officer phrased it. When he figured out what was going on, my mother started begging him for money as she was climbing on top of him trying to seduce him. She wanted the money in payment for her sexual services to get a hit.

She then started hallucinating and thought that the neighbor's boyfriend was some animal trying to fight her when he was simply trying to restrain her. She then began to fight him and in the process, vandalize the house. My neighbor called the police after she got in a few punches herself, while her boyfriend restrained my mother.

When the police came, she said she wanted to press charges. I came out of my room as the officer finished explaining things to my aunt.

He handed me my phone.

"You're lucky that you have such a concerned aunt. I'll wait with you until she gets here."

"I know my mother is going to jail," I said.

"Well, Ms. Lawson, your mother is highly intoxicated and she needs help."

I broke down in tears again. I had been waiting for my mother to get help for so long. Maybe this would be her chance.

"It's going to be okay. Here," he said handing me his card. "You can call me on Monday. That way I can tell you what's going to happen to her after she has been processed in the system."

All of a sudden I heard my neighbor scream, "Get that crazy bitch out of here!"

The officer and I ran to the front porch and saw my neighbor rush to the cop car and start clawing at my mother's leg. The officer who was already outside tried to pull my neighbor away. My mother was still screaming and was kicking at her. It was too much for me to take.

"Wait inside for you aunt. Let me go help out," the officer that was waiting with me said.

It seemed like hours before my aunt got there. The police got the situation under control just as Aunt Lena ran into the house.

"Mimi, let's get out of here!" she said. I was so glad that she came to save me. She slammed the front door shut and locked it. She held me to her chest as we walked to the car. She was trying to make sure that I couldn't see my mother. But my mother saw me as they escorted her to another patrol car.

"Mia! Mia! I'm sorry!"

I didn't feel an ounce of sympathy. I was numb.

"Lena! Thank you for taking my princess with you. Mia! I love you!"

The officer pushed my mother's head down to help her get in the back of the car.

"Are you okay?" Mookie asked as I got in the back seat. I could see my mother crying hysterically and yelling my name as the police car drove off.

"I'm all right," I said as I processed the whole event. "Just get me the hell away from here."

Chapter 6

I RUBBED MY EYES, GRATEFUL FOR THE NEW DAY, BUT NOT READY TO GET up yet.

"What time is it?" I asked.

"Yeah…yeah, I'll catch you later," I heard Mookie say as he ended his phone call. "What's up, cuz? You sleep okay?"

"Yeah, the best in a while," I said yawning and stretching.

Mookie got out of the chair and sat on the bed next to me. "You lucky you're my cousin, I would have never let anyone else sleep in my bed and make me take the floor."

I looked at the floor and saw the blankets and pillows. "Man, I'm sorry Mook; you didn't have to do that."

"Yeah, well like I said, you're lucky I like you," he said as he winked at me.

I looked at my cousin and noticed that he was starting to grow facial hair and that he was looking more mature. He had been working out more lately and it was no wonder he couldn't keep the girls off of him. Muscles bulged from his arms and in the ripples on his chest. He had the same smooth caramel skin and hazel eyes as my mom, Aunt Lena, and me.

"I know last night was crazy. You sure you okay?"

"Yeah, I'll come out on top as usual," I said. "Where is Auntie?"

"She went to church. You know she spends all day there so I guess it's just me and you today."

"Cool. Got any plans?"

"Maybe. Why don't you get yourself together? Mama said that you are staying with us for a while, so I guess I have to take you to get some things from your house this week."

My cousin and I spent the rest of the afternoon chilling' at the house. Marissa called to see how I was doing. We talked for a while and she told me that the whole block was worried about me. Apparently my mother's drug problems were not as much of a secret as I would have liked them to be.

Aunt Lena came home that afternoon and began cooking a huge Sunday dinner.

"Your mom called this morning, Mimi."

"Great. What did she want?" I asked without any enthusiasm.

"She has court for her charges in the morning. I'm going to go. You two may have to go to family court on Wednesday depending on what the judge says tomorrow. Mimi, I hope they send her to rehab because she really needs help. In the meanwhile, she agreed to sign over temporary custody of you to me. Do you want to go to court with me?"

Hell no! I thought to myself. I had been through enough. I needed some time to myself. "No thanks, Auntie. I think I'll let you handle it. I've had enough of my mother for a while. I'm glad to be staying here. What about school?"

"I'll get the temporary custody so that I can take all of your paperwork and enroll you in school. Only thing is you'll be in school over here, though."

"I kinda figured that. It's cool. I can make friends anywhere." I sighed, as for a brief moment, the thought crossed my mind that my father should be the one to take care of me if my mother couldn't. That wasn't Aunt Lena's responsibility, it was his. But who knew where his ass was. All I could do was give Aunt Lena a hug. She held me tightly as I cried. I couldn't stop the tears from falling. As much as I tried to act like this whole thing wasn't bothering me, it was eating me alive.

Aunt Lena got dressed and went with one of her co-workers to a comedy club for the evening. I had never really seen her go out for fun. Mookie told me to get dressed because he had to go take care of some business. I got dressed quickly, ready to get out of the house.

"I'm ready," I called down the hallway.

"You wearin' that?" Mookie asked with his face frowned up. I looked at my clothes; a white wife beater, blue jean skirt with rhinestones outlining the pockets, and white Air force ones. I didn't see the problem.

"Yeah, and?"

"Mimi, you look-,"

"*Look* what?" I interrupted. I know he wasn't trippin' about my clothes.

He sucked his teeth. I could tell he wanted to say something, but he was holding back.

"Like what, Mookie? Like one of the chicks out there that you holla at? I am sixteen and it's not my fault I look good. It's in my genes," I tried to joke. I had never seen Mookie so uptight.

"I guess," he answered. "I just never noticed that you had all of that," he said pointing at my behind. "And all of that," he said, pointing at my chest.

"Well, what do you want me to do, Mook? I could put on a baggy pair of sweats and dudes would still try to get with me."

"Whatever," he snapped. "You're my little cousin. I gotta watch out for you."

"I do pretty good on my own. Now let's go."

We got in the car. When the car started, the Big Tymers CD blasted through the speakers. I ejected the CD and inserted my Gangta Boo "Both Worlds *69" CD. Mookie looked at me funny. He was never really into female MCs.

"Don't start Mookie. Gangsta Boo is one of the realest female MCs out there. She's tight. Just listen." I turned on track 14 and started bobbing my head with the music. Soon he did too.

"Where are we going?" I asked.

"Look, just sit back and ride. I got a stop to make and I need you to just sit in the car while I do something."

We rolled to Cleveland Ave in East Point. Mookie pulled up to a small ranch style house. "I'll be right back. Don't move," he said.

I sat back in the car and turned on the radio. I bobbed my head to the song playing and sang the lyrics. I took a drink of some of my water as I waited for my cousin to come back out of the house. A big man had answered the door and invited him in.

As I leaned my head back to take a drink, I spilled some of the water. I hated it when I missed my mouth. "Shit!" I said, as I laughed at myself. I let myself out of the car, still holding the bottle of water, to wipe some of the water off of my clothes. A black Benz pulled up alongside of me.

"You always miss your mouth like that?"

I looked up to see a tall, sexy man laughing at me as he double parked his car and walked over to me.

"Damn, you saw me?"

"Yeah, I'm glad that I did though. You looking' good, Lil' Mama," he said as his eyes ran up and down my body.

"You too," I said. "What's your name?"

"Mark. And what's yours?"

"Mia."

"So what's up Mia? Can I get your number?"

I looked behind him to see if Mookie was on his way out of the house. I'd hate for him to come out and start clownin'.

"Yeah," I started to get that same hot feeling between my legs that I did when I saw Brian. "You live around here?"

"No, one of my partners lives up the street. When I saw you standin' out here, I had to stop and talk to you."

"Well, look, let me give you my number. I'm waiting on my cousin."

Mark put my number in his cell phone and I put his in mine. He told me he would call me later and drove off.

Just as I got back in the car, Mookie walked out of the house. A large man walked out onto the porch. Smoke rose from his cigar as he gave Mookie some dap. He looked old enough to be Mookie's father and I wondered what kind of business he could be taking care of.

Mookie ran back to the car as the man walked back into the house.

"Who is that?" I asked.

"I should ask you the same thing. I saw you talking to some dude, Mimi. I thought I told you to stay in the car!"

"Mookie, the last time I checked, you were only my cousin, not my daddy. Stop trippin'!"

He looked at me and sucked his teeth as he drove off. We sat in silence until we hit I-85 and cruised through the city. He still hadn't said who the man was or what we were doing at his house.

Mookie looked over at me while I was still waiting for him to tell me what was up.

"That man was a friend of my dad's," he blurted out.

"What!" I said. I turned the radio down to see if I had heard him correctly.

"You heard me. He is a friend of my dad's."

"Does Aunt Lena know about him?"

"No, Mia and she won't know." I know Mookie meant business because he called me by my name. "Look, his name is Troy. He was my dad's best friend. He's the one that gave my mom all of my dad's money when he died. I ran into him one day downtown and I decided to keep in touch with him."

We all knew that Mookie's dad was involved in any and everything illegal. He sold drugs, ran scams, whatever hustle paid the bills. It was mostly the drugs though and that led to him being killed.

"Mookie, is this dude straight? I mean, is he legit?"

"No, Mia. And that doesn't matter to me." Mookie just looked straight ahead as he drove. I could tell that I was pissing him off. He was trying to keep something from me and I felt like that something was not good news.

"Mimi, I never knew my dad. Then I'm downtown one day and this brother walks up to me and tells me that I've got to be Big Rob's kid because I look just like him. I always thought that I looked just like Mama. Troy gives me his number and says to keep in touch. I call him up and go by one day after I came by to see you and Aunt Tricie. He shows me pictures of my dad and I do look like him. I felt like I had missed out on so much.

"Mama tells me some things about my dad, but not much. She hardly has any pictures of him and she doesn't talk about him. She says that she wants to move on and that part of her life is over. She doesn't realize that I need to know about him because it's a part of me that I never knew and I'll never know. Troy is cool peoples and he's gonna help me with this music thing. He owns a studio and I'm gonna go and lay some tracks next week."

"Oh yeah? That's aight I guess. I'm just concerned because you really don't know this Troy. He could be trouble."

"And so could that lil' dude that you just exchanged numbers wit!"

"Damn, Mookie! Why you trippin' on me like this? You never used to act like that!"

"Excuse me for being concerned about you, Mimi! These kids out here ain't got nothin' for you! You need to concentrate on school and do somethin' wit yourself!"

I sighed loudly as I sat with my arms crossed. I didn't know where this was coming from. "I get all A's in school for your information! And maybe you wouldn't trip if you didn't treat girls the way you do. I see the way they fall all over you and you run through them like water! What? You don't want somebody to treat me like you treat girls?"

Mookie rubbed his hand across his forehead. We sat in silence again for a while. I turned up the radio to drown out the silence. I was hoping that he was taking the time out to get over himself.

We pulled up to Aunt Lena's house. It didn't look like she was home yet.

"Mimi, I apologize. It's just been hard lately when we hang out to see the way that men look at you. Because you live wit' me now, I feel like I really need to protect you even more. I feel like I'm gonna have to kill somebody over you. I mean, I would probably get at you if you weren't my little cuz." We laughed at his comment as he reached over and hugged me.

"You got to trust me, Mookie. I don't get around like that."

"Good. And this thing about me talking with Troy, I don't want Mama to know yet. I have a feeling she'll really flip on me if she finds out."

"Fine. I won't tell."

I agreed to keep his secret for now. The image of Troy on the porch giving Mookie daps flashed in my mind. There had to be some other reason that Mookie didn't want Aunt Lena to know that he met up with Troy. I just hoped that this Troy was not going to be trouble for my cousin. God knows that my mother had already caused enough trouble for the family.

Chapter 7

I FOUND OUT THAT I WOULD BE SPENDING THE REST OF THE SCHOOL YEAR at Aunt Lena's. My mother went to court and the judge ordered that she go to rehab for thirty days and then a halfway house for six months. The judge also gave Aunt Lena temporary custody of me because she said that no one knew where my father was and that he hadn't been in my life for the past six years. I was grateful for that because Aunt Lena and Mookie had become the only other family that I knew.

Mark and I hit it off immediately. He was older than me - 22 years old to be exact. I know that his age could be a problem for some people, but after all that I had been through, I was a little more mature for my age. We talked about everything. I told him all about my family life and all he did was listen. He didn't care that my family was fucked up and I let it slide that he was a hustler.

Mark showered me with gifts and affection that I hadn't known before. I had new tennis shoes every other week, new jewelry. He spoiled me like I was supposed to be spoiled. We were out one day and Mark took me past my house to get some more of my things. I asked him to wait outside for me. The truth was that I wanted to go inside my house alone and take some time out.

I was glad that we still had the house. Aunt Lena said that my father had paid it off and that she would pay the utilities to keep everything going until my mom came home. I thought about it and realized that paying the house off was one of the best things that my dad had ever done for us. Sometimes I wished that he would keep in touch, other times I hoped that he would stay right where he was.

The phone rang as I was on the way out of the door.

"Hey girl, I see you big timin' now!"

"Not exactly," I answered. It could only be Marissa's nosy ass.

"I saw you when you pulled up. What's up?"

Marissa and I talked for a minute and I told her about Mark. Then she deflated my good feeling and brought up her brother. "You know, he knows we still talk and he asks about you all the time."

I wanted to be over Brian, but it was hard. He was my first. But if he only knew how Mark was puttin' that thang on me.

"Yeah, well, me and Brian are over. I moved on. Are you still coming to Aunt Lena's for Labor Day weekend?"

"Hell yeah! Is your cousin still fine?"

"Keep your legs closed, 'ho'! He's with some other chick right now."

"He wouldn't be if he knew what was good for him," she answered, with a giggle.

Marissa and I talked for a minute more when I heard Mark blow the horn.

"Guess that's your cue. I'll catch you later girl. I miss you around the block."

"I miss you too. But I'll see you on the holiday."

We hung up and I raced outside and got in the car.

"You sure took a long time," Mark said. If I had thought about it, it seemed like he was questioning me.

"Yeah, well, I miss being home."

"Yeah, whatever," he said blowing me off.

We drove toward the highway and he suggested that we go back to his crib. It was cool with me. I reminded him that I had to be back kind of early so that I could get ready for the first day of school.

When we got to Mark's crib, we chilled out on the couch and turned on the television. He dropped a dime sack of weed and some blunt paper on the table. Mark went to the kitchen and returned with a jar of grape jelly. I looked at him puzzled.

"The jelly makes it taste sweet when you smoke it." I shrugged. I had lived my life around people who sold or used drugs and I never really took any interest. With Mark, for some reason, I wanted to get into everything that he was doing. I figured one blunt wouldn't hurt.

He showed me how to roll a joint and how to smoke it. I don't know if I liked it or not, but I guess that didn't matter by the time that I had lit the third one. In between we had the most amazing sex that we had ever had. He had me doing things that I never thought were possible. After the last blunt, I realized that I was the one who was high and Mark seemed like the weed hadn't affected him at all.

My head was floating on cloud nine and I felt so laid back and relaxed. I wasn't ready to leave but I figured that I needed to so that I could get ready for school. I called my Aunt so that she wouldn't be worried about me and I told her that I was on my way home. When she answered her cell, she said that she was on her way to work for some overtime. I was relieved because I was high as shit and I didn't want her to catch me.

Mark dropped me off and Mookie met me at the door. I had put on my sunglasses so that my cousin couldn't see that I was blazed.

"Mimi, who was that? He looks old as shit. How old is he?" Mookie asked as I came through the door.

"He's nineteen," I lied. "He just looks mature."

"And I guess his parents are rich and that's why he drives that Benz."

"You know what, I could always let Aunt Lena know that you are keeping company with Troy!"

"Whatever, Mimi," he answered. "Did you run wild like this at home?"

I just twisted up my face and walked toward my room. His crazy ass followed me. He was blowing my high.

"What, Mookie? I have to get my clothes ready for school." He grabbed me and pulled me up to him.

"I smell the weed on you, Mimi! I can't believe you! After all of this with your mother, you go out and smoke some of that shit!"

I struggled to pull myself free from his grip. I hadn't noticed how strong my cousin was. It took me a second, but I got free of his grip.

"Mookie, give me a break! Okay, I had one blunt, but it's not my thing," I lied.

"It better not be. My cousin better not be getting' high!"

"When did you become Mr. High and Mighty, Mookie?"

"Mimi, you obviously need someone to look out for you. I don't like that Mark. Why hasn't he come up here and introduced himself?"

"I'm not ready to introduce him yet. It's not that serious yet," I said, as I started getting my clothes together for the next day. I just wanted him to leave me alone. He had been on me lately and it was getting on my nerves. He just better keep his mouth shut though.

Mookie finally got the point that I wasn't talking to him and went back to his own room. Who was he to talk about what I was doing when he had so many girls running in and out of this house at night, when Aunt Lena was at work. that it was ridiculous? And it was a different girl almost every night. It was like he was fucking all of the Eastside.

Aunt Lena came home early and she had breakfast cooked for us to start out on our first day of school. It was cool. My mom had never done that. Mookie took his books out to the car to wait for me because I was late as usual.

"Mimi, wait a minute," said Aunt Lena. "I just want you to know that I'm glad that I could be here for you. All I ask is that you go to school and do your best. I know things are real messed up right now, but Patrice is going to get through this. I love you both so much. We are going to get past this and things will be better for all of us." Aunt Lena gave me a kiss on the cheek and I felt for a minute that things would work out for the best. My Aunt Lena told me so and she never lied.

Chapter 8

My mom was released from rehab after successfully completing the thirty-day program. She asked me to come by and see her before she went to the halfway house. I couldn't do it. It was all just too much. I felt like I had been abandoned twice; first my dad and then her. I wanted to try to focus on myself for once. Hell, my parents had focused on themselves during my entire life. Why couldn't I take the time out for myself now?

School was all right, but I didn't make as many friends as I had made at my own school. It sucked being the new student during my junior year. I became known as "Mookie's cousin." The girls were all too jealous acting for me, and the boys were not on my level. What could they offer me when I was dating a grown man?

Despite Mookie's continued protesting, I still was with Mark. I didn't see the problem. Mark had become my escape from everything. When I was with him, I could forget all of the other shit going on in my life. I had all of these feelings about the situation with my parents and I felt like I would never get to a place of peace.

I was doing well in school despite everything, so I suggested that I take a day off of school when Mark came to pick me up that morning. He took me to school most days and picked me up every afternoon.

We went over to his house to kick it. We started our usual ritual of getting high and having a drink. I had taken to smoking weed a lot more often. It relaxed me and I felt like I could think more clearly. Things were cool and then his phone rang. I wouldn't have minded until I saw his facial expression change. It was obvious that he was talking to some other chick. I was high, so I played it cool as I listened to his conversation and vibed to the music.

"Yeah, so come on by and kick it wit' us... Cool. I'll see you in a few."

He ended the phone conversation like it was nothing.

"Who the fuck was that Mark?" I said, as I sat up on the end of the couch. I couldn't believe that he would invite some other broad over to his house like that, especially while I was there.

Mark took another hit of the weed and exhaled as he sat back and listened to the music.

"Why you trippin' Mia? I ain't never seen you trip. That's one of the main reasons why I like you."

"Yeah, well, I know you were on the phone wit' some other chick. What's up?"

"Oh her? That was Simone. She's cool," he said as he continued to smoke. He passed me the blunt. I took another hit.

"Why is she comin' over? I thought we were chillin' today?" *And who the hell was Simone anyway? Why does she know how to get to your house?*

"Look, me and her been cool for a minute. Since before you and me met. She knows about us. I just thought maybe we could all chill this afternoon. Here have a drink," Mark said as he passed me a wine cooler. He always bought me wine coolers because he said that I was too young to drink.

I took a sip and another hit of the blunt to calm my nerves. I needed to know who this Simone was. Mark acted like everything was cool. He leaned over and started kissing me on the neck. I gave in to his touch like always. The knock at the door interrupted us.

"Why don't you go back to the bedroom and get sexy for me? I'll be back there in a minute."

Good. He got the point and was going to get rid of this Simone chick and the two of us could chill for the day. I went to the bedroom and changed into my red lace teddy and matching thong.

I heard laughing and the front door closed. I turned on some music to set the mood and lit the candles that were around the bed. I turned off the lights and got ready for my man.

"Damn, girl, I'm glad you're ready for me."

I looked up and saw two people walk through the door. Mark closed the door as he walked the woman over to the bed. She was gorgeous; tall and thin, long legs and very busty. She had smooth coco skin, round eyes and a small nose. When she smiled, she showed perfect white teeth. She wore her hair up in a loose upsweep. She walked in and took her overcoat off and revealed a black lace negligee that showed off everything.

"Mia, this is Simone. Simone, this is my girl, Mia."

"She's cute Mark," she said as she ran her hand down the side of his face giggling. "Hey doll," she said, as she licked her lips at me.

It suddenly dawned on me through my purple haze that Mark was trying to have a threesome. I had never ever thought about being with another woman and being a lesbian was not my thing.

My heart started racing. I couldn't believe Mark had me trapped like this. What was I going to do? Get up and leave? Mark would definitely think that I was a little girl if I did that. I couldn't let this Simone come in and take my man. She was obviously down for anything and it didn't look like she was leaving anytime soon.

She started moving her body to the music. Mark left to go to the kitchen and get some drinks for all of us. Simone was lost in her own world. I guess she was already intoxicated.

Mark came back in the room with a tray of whipped cream, strawberries, and ice. It suddenly became hot in the room as I realized that the heat had come on. Mark sat the tray down.

"Is that for me?" Simone asked as she pointed to the tray.

"All for you," he said. Simone went over to the tray and I realized that she wasn't talking about the food. She reached for the razor and cut two lines of cocaine. She snorted like a pro and sat up looking refreshed.

"You cool with this Mia? I mean, you don't have to if you don't want to," Mark said.

I knew that he was trying me. If I said that I wasn't down, he would get with this Simone more often and I would be left out in the cold. I wasn't about to let that happen. She wasn't taking Mark from me.

"Yeah, I'm fine. But I'm not doin' the coke."

"That wasn't for you anyway, Mia. Simone likes it. She says that it gets her ready."

"Ready for what?" I asked, eyebrow raised. It sounded like too much experience between Mark and Simone.

"Come on, Mia. Don't be a baby. You want to be a grown woman, act like it. You know what's up. So either you're down or you're not," he whispered to me.

It only took me a quick second. I was grown and I was going to prove it.

"Is it time to get the party started?" Simone asked. I could see a thin layer of sweat forming on her skin from the heat in the room. Mark said that it turned him on to have sex in the room while it was hot and see the sweat glisten on my body. She walked over to me as I sat on the bed and pulled me up to her. She lightly planted a kiss on my lips. It was weird, but it was similar to kissing a man. I could smell her perfume as she leaned in closer to me. She kissed me again and I saw Mark smiling at us out the corner of my eye. He was enjoying himself.

The next thing I know, Simone had her hands between my legs, touching me lightly. I couldn't believe that it got my juices going. Simone let out a soft moan and leaned me back on the bed. Mark came over and began watching. I was trying to make myself think that I wasn't enjoying this, but I was. I don't know if it was the fact that I smoked and drank a little bit before, or if it was that I wanted to make Mark happy.

Simone pulled down my teddy and spread whipped cream all over my breasts. I saw her look back and wink at Mark. By now, he had taken off his clothes and joined us on the bed. They each took a breast in their mouths and began licking and sucking while Simone continued to tease my middle with her fingers. I couldn't lie, the pleasure was intense.

We continued and I was surprised that I let Simone do the things to me that she did. Soon, she was licking my middle as Mark hit her from behind. We all changed positions so that Mark had a chance to get with both of us. Simone knew that I didn't want to do any tasting her, so she played it cool and didn't trip over it.

All I could say was that there was a lot of licking and sucking and a whole lot of sex going down on those satin sheets. After we were all satisfied, I lay down next to Mark as Simone went to the bathroom to clean herself up. She came out and put her coat back on.

"Later, Mark. Later, doll," she said winking at me. "I enjoyed myself as usual Mark. I'll let myself out." She left the room and I heard the front door close. Mark went and turned the heat down so that we could get comfortable.

As he ran bathwater for us in the garden tub of his master bathroom, I laid there trying to process what had just happened. I had just had a *ménage a trois* for my man.

Mark came out of the bathroom and motioned that the bath water was ready.

"So, you aight?" he asked as he washed my back.

"I'm cool," I responded.

"Mia, you're always cool. You really okay? I know I just kind of sprung that whole thing on you."

"I'm fine, Mark."

"That's my good girl," he said as he kissed my neck. There was no way that he was going anywhere after I just did that for him.

After spending the afternoon together, Mark took me home. When I got there, I saw that Mookie had beaten me home. Aunt Lena's car was in the driveway. I asked Mark to circle the block and come back and let me out a couple blocks down.

He did. When I walked into the house, Aunt Lena was in the kitchen and Mookie was sitting on the couch in the living room. He shook his head at me. I rolled my eyes and put my books down on the dining room table.

"What's up, Aunt Lena?" I said.

"I don't know Mia. What's up with you? How was school?"

"Good. The usual. Nothing exciting."

"Really?" Aunt Lena questioned.

"Yeah, why?" I asked, as I went to get a drink out of the refrigerator.

"Maybe you can explain why the school called and said that you were absent today?"

I looked over at Mookie. He just shrugged his shoulders. I know that mofo didn't tell on me. He couldn't have. He read my mind and mouthed the words 'I didn't tell her'.

"Mia, I can't believe that you skipped school like that!" Aunt Lena said in disgust. "What did you do all day, Mia?"

Aunt Lena and Mookie looked at me waiting for my answer. *Let's see, I skipped school, got high, and had a threesome with my man and some other chick.*

"I just took the train home to my house, Auntie. I wanted to take some time out to get my head together. I honestly haven't taken the time to think things through after Mama got out of rehab. I don't know. I'm sorry. I should have just called you and told you that I wanted to take a day off." Wow! I amazed myself that I could lie that quickly on demand.

I looked over at Mookie and I could tell that he knew I was full of shit. He started coughing loudly. Aunt Lena and I looked over at him. He played it off like he was choking.

"I'm fine," he said waving his hand and taking a drink. Aunt Lena turned back to me. I looked quickly back at my cousin who mouthed the words 'bullshit'. I rolled my eyes and turned back to my aunt.

"Mimi, this whole thing is hard for me too. But your mom is getting the help that she needs to get her life together. She is trying. She misses you and wants to hear from you, but she can understand if you don't want to speak to her.

"Look, I know there are going to be times that you need to vent or take some time out. I'm fine with that, but I refuse to see a smart girl like you mess up because her parents fucked up. You are so close to finishing school. I will not watch you mess yourself up.

I'm here for you and you know that. I just want what's best for you and that right now is to finish and focus on your education. You got that?"

"Yes, Auntie. I'm sorry."

Aunt Lena walked over and gave me a hug. As I looked over her shoulder, Mookie mouthed the words 'full of shit'. I stuck my tongue out at him and rolled my eyes again. I knew what my Aunt Lena said was true. I knew that she would always be there for me. But what she didn't know was that I had Mark too, and I wasn't letting go of him for anything.

Chapter 9

AFTER THE THREESOME, I TRIED TO CONVINCE MYSELF THAT MARK WASN'T acting strangely. But he was. He wasn't coming to get me as often because, he said, he had business to take care of. It was for the best though, because I needed some time to go over in my head what went down that day.

I wondered if I was losing it. I never would have thought that I would go that far for a man. I had to admit to myself that sleeping with Mark and another woman was never on my agenda when I said that I wanted to chill with him for the day.

It kind of pissed me off that he didn't ask me about if I was down before he invited Simone over. And what was that about anyway? First she calls and then she's there in seconds like she was already on her way over. It was almost like it didn't even matter if I was there or not. She had on lingerie under a coat so she was coming to get hers, regardless, I guess. I wasn't even smart or sober enough to see the game plan from the start.

The fact that she was obviously older than me made me feel insecure. She and Mark were probably the same age. She didn't look like the type that came to his house, or anybody's house for that matter, = to just kick it. She was some "cut" without a doubt. It was killing me that she and Mark had obviously been together before, and it didn't seem like they stopped since I came into the picture.

I found myself daydreaming about Mark in school. I couldn't figure out why he had this pull on me. What did he want with me anyway? He was fine as shit and he could have any girl that he wanted and here he was chillin' with me. The other day was the first time that my age seemed to make a difference to him. He was practically calling me a baby if I wasn't going to participate. I decided that while he was handling business, it would be best if I concentrated on school. I had been doing pretty well, all things considered, and I wanted to impress Aunt Lena with my grades at midterm report.

The phone rang one evening before Aunt Lena left for work. She glanced at me as she spoke.

"Yeah, let me see. Mia," she said holding her hand over the receiver as she whispered. "It's your mother. She would love to speak to you."

I sat on the couch and flipped through a couple more channels before I acknowledged her.

"Come on Mimi, just talk to her for a second. She's doing well. She's better." She stretched the phone toward me. I sighed heavily as I got up off the couch.

I grabbed the phone. "Hello," I said informally.

"Mimi? It's Mama. Hey baby!"

There was an uncomfortable silence. The sound of her voice tugged at my heart. I swallowed hard, trying to keep it together.

"Mimi, I don't have long on the phone. I just wanted you to know that I'm doing well and I'm going to come home to you a clean woman. I know I fucked up big time. I want to work hard to get things back together for us. I want you to forgive me, of course in time, and I would like to be a better mother to you. I love you Mimi."

My mother had just poured her heart out to me and I wasn't sure what I was supposed to say in response to her.

"Okay, Mama," was all I managed. I loved my mother, but I didn't want her making false promises over the phone and then coming home and tearing my world apart again.

I passed the phone back to Aunt Lena and went back to my bedroom. I heard Aunt Lena end the phone call with my mom and tell her that she should give me some time.

I turned on my TV and watched music videos while I tried to drown my feelings. Aunt Lena peeked her head in the door.

"Mimi, I'm going to work now and Mookie should be home from work soon. You all right?"

"Yeah, Auntie. I'm fine," I said, as I continued to stare at the screen.

"Well, I might have to work an extra hour in the morning so tell Mookie that I won't be off until eight."

"Alright. Later Auntie."

I heard the garage door close and her car pull off. My phone rang. Mark's name flashed across the cell phone screen.

"What's up, Lil' Mama?"

"Not much," I said through a smile. I was glad that he had called.

"I was going to come by and scoop you up."

"Sounds cool. I'll be ready."

I found my biggest purse and packed an extra outfit and grabbed my toothbrush. I planned on staying the night at Mark's and leaving for school from there. I stopped for a minute and wondered if Mookie would snitch on me. I laughed at the thought because I could always tell Auntie how he had all those hoochies coming over and calling when she went to work at night. I knew he wasn't telling.

Mark and I got to his crib, ordered some pizza and watched a movie. I started falling asleep when he told me he would take me home.

"I thought that I would stay the night." I waited for his response. He smiled at me and shook his head.

"You sure about that?"

"Yeah. My aunt works overnight from seven at night until seven in the morning and tomorrow, she gets off late. She's usually not even there when you pick me up for school. She's working an extra hour in the morning, so I'm straight."

We kicked it the rest of the night, no sex. Mark even told me about some of his 'business deals'. I felt special because he was actually sharing things with me. I told him about things with my mom and me.

"No wonder you always trying' to hang wit' me. But you can't run from things Mia. The world is 360 degrees and shit always catches back up to you. You gotta deal wit' things."

It sounded a bit philosophical. It was a side of Mark that I had never seen.

I called Mookie when I knew he was off work and told him that I was staying out. He tried to trip, but I reminded him about his revolving door of 'hoes' and it shut him up quickly.

The next morning, I decided that I wanted to stay home from school. The school hadn't called my aunt the last two times that I skipped, so I figured that I would be cool.

We lay around all morning, even having breakfast in bed. Mark got up to get a shower because he had some things to do that day. He told me I could chill at his house until he took me home.

While he was out, the phone rang more than it ever had since I had known him. When it rang for the fifth time, I answered as a reflex. I couldn't stand to let the phone just ring.

"Hello?"

"Ma- who the fuck is this?" the voice demanded.

"His girl! Who is this? You called here!"

"Where is Mark?" the voice asked in between sucking teeth.

"Why? Who the hell are you?" *Who the hell was she that she thought she could talk to me like that?*

"Look bitch! I asked for Mark, not you! I'll just hit his cell!"

She hung up. My anger had me speechless. First Simone, now this. I had tried to convince myself that Simone was nothing, but this bitch that just called was trying to pull rank and I wasn't having it.

Mark walked through the door right at 3:30; when I should have been coming home from school.

"Mia, what did you do?" he said, as he slammed the front door.

I sucked my teeth. I know he wasn't questioning me after he had some other bitch calling for him.

"Who was the bitch calling Mark?"

"What the hell were you doing answering my phone?"

"What? I'm your girl, Mark! You shouldn't have anything to hide from me!"

Mark shook his head. "Mia, get your shit. I need to take you home. And when did you become 'my girl' like that enough to answer my house phone?"

All I could do was stand there with my mouth open. I couldn't believe what he had just said. I snapped out of it and ran to get my things. The ride home was quiet and I was glad that he didn't live far from Aunt Lena's.

My cell phone rang a couple times, but I ignored it. I was fuming.

"Aren't you gonna answer that?" he asked.

"No. I caught hell the last time I answered a phone," I said sarcastically as I sank back in my seat.

"Mia, I thought you got our relationship. I mean, we're cool but I thought you understood the fact that you and me just kick it. That's all. I don't want a girlfriend or any of that shit. I'm too young and I got too much goin' on to have a girl now. I got shit to do and I can't be thinking about you."

I had to laugh. That's what I get for picking another hustler. Brian told me the same thing.

"You sure it's not my age, Mark?"

He just sighed as he turned the corner for my street. "I'm not gonna lie. I could get locked up for fuckin' wit' you. But I dig you and I like your company. I just can't take you trippin' like I'm kickin' it wit just you."

Bam! There it was. The truth smacking me in the face. He had just put the ball in my court and it was up to me to decide what I was going to do with it.

"Look Mia, take some time out. I gotta go out of town for a few. I'll call you when I get back."

"Don't bother. I think you've said enough."

He stopped the car a few houses down like usual. I didn't even say anything else when I got out of the car. He just shook his head and drove off.

My phone chimed again and I saw it was a text message from Mookie. What the hell did he want?

Mama came home early today. Knows u cut school. U R N deep shit!

Shit! What happened to working an extra hour? Great! That was all I needed. I might as well go and take my punishment. I didn't want to make my aunt mad at me, but I wasn't in the mood for what was going to go down with her after what happened with Mark.

I walked through the door; Aunt Lena was standing there waiting for me. As soon as I put my key in the door and turned the knob, she snatched the door open.

"What the fuck, Mia!"

"Auntie I-," I didn't get any more words out before she grabbed me by my shirt. I had no idea that she was so strong.

"I thought I told you that you were supposed to be at school! What the hell were you doing, Mia?"

I knew that was a trick question. Nothing I could say would be the correct answer. I dropped my bag and tried to free myself from her grasp, but this caused her to twist my shirt tighter.

"Answer me, Mia!"

"Auntie, I'm sorry!"

She shoved me away from her and let go of her grasp. I stumbled backwards; the only thing that helped me to catch my balance was the couch. I tried to straighten my shirt and get myself together.

Where the hell was Mookie? I had never seen my aunt flip like this and I needed some reinforcement.

"Sorry is not going to work Mia!" she screamed. She was on me again. This time she was in my face. We were practically nose-to-nose.

"And I know you're fuckin' that boy that drops you off and picks you up all the time with your hot ass! You think I don't know about his grown ass! I seen him, Mia! I should call the police and have his ass locked up for statutory rape. You are sixteen! You are not grown!"

Shit! I never thought that she knew anything. I thought I was
smart enough to keep him far enough away.

"And if you want to know, Mookie didn't tell me about him!
I'm a grown ass woman, not to mention a mother that knows these
things Mia!" He was lucky she said that. I was about to let loose
about Mookie's nightly Freaknik at the house if he had been the
one to snitch.

I opened my mouth to defend myself and I thought again.
Aunt Lena's eyes were spitting fire and I was already getting burned.

"I can't believe you would come here Mia and disrespect my
house like this!" she said as she walked away from me. She started
pacing the floor as she continued ranting. I was not about to move
for fear of what she would do next.

"I can't look at you right now, Mia! I need you to go to your
room and close the door and I don't want to see you until I'm
ready. I need some time so that I don't put my hands around your
neck and strangle the life out of you right now!"

I took my cue and slid past her as she continued to zap out in
the living room. I heard Mookie in his room watching TV through
his closed door. I closed my door gently, not trying to let it slam
and give her a reason to come and take my life. I had to admit that
was some scary shit. I never imagined that she could flip like that.

My cell phone rang and I answered without looking at the
caller ID.

"You fucked up, cuz!"

Leave it to Mookie to rub it in.

"I guess so. I never seen her like that before."

"Yeah, well, neither have I and she's my mother. I guess I'm in
for the night because I'm not leaving this room for anything. I'm
not catching an ass whipping' because you fucked up!"

I had to laugh. He was right. The way Aunt Lena looked, she
was ready to kick ass and it didn't seem like it mattered whose ass
it was.

"I didn't tell on you either."

"I know, Mook. Thanks. Besides, I think that whole relationship is pretty much over anyway. I'm glad you looked out for me. I'm sorry that I wasn't seeing things clearly."

"What are you talkin' about? He didn't do anything to you, did he!"

"No! Calm down! I just had to realize some things on my own. I see now. I need to move on from him." My other line beeped. I saw that it was Marissa calling.

"Look, we'll talk later. That's Marissa. And no, I won't tell her you said what's up."

"Whatever, cuz," Mookie said, as he laughed.

I clicked over and chatted with Marissa for a minute. I told her about all of the shit I was in.

"Damn girl, you fucked up! You better apologize with the quickness. Aunt Lena is all you got."

"I know. I really didn't mean to make her mad." I could still hear her in the living room pacing around and fussing.

I heard the doorbell ring. I continued to talk to Marissa about how things were back in the hood. She filled me in with all the latest gossip.

The front door opened and the screen door slammed.

I heard Aunt Lena say "Long time no see."

I couldn't imagine who was out there. I just continued to talk to Marissa and hope that whoever it was could help calm Aunt Lena down.

"Mia, get out here now. There is someone here for you!"

"Girl, let me go. I don't want to keep Auntie waiting. I'm not tryin' to get my ass kicked."

"I know, that's right!" Marissa giggled.

"I'll call you later," I said, as I hung up.

"Yes Auntie!" I answered. I opened the bedroom door and walked down the hall to the living room. I couldn't believe my eyes. My heart started racing and I thought that my bladder was going to release itself as I stood frozen. I blinked my eyes again just to make sure that I wasn't seeing things.

"Mimi!" he said as he held his arms out to me. I couldn't move. I didn't know if I was paralyzed with fear or if it was because I couldn't take one more thing happening in my day today.

The last thing I said before I fainted and hit the floor was his name.

"Daddy."

Chapter 10

"MIMI! GIRL, WAKE UP!"

I felt the light tapping of someone's fingers and the cool cloth on my face. Aunt Lena, being the nurse she was, brushed some smelling salts past my nose. I came to, not remembering how I got to the point where I was laid out on the floor. Had Aunt Lena really taken me out after being mad at me?

"Auntie, what happened?" I asked as I rubbed my head. She helped me as I tried to sit up. Things were very cloudy and the room was spinning slightly. I leaned on her for support as she helped me over to the dining room table to sit down. As my dad came out of the kitchen and handed me a glass of water, I remembered why I had hit the floor.

"Are you okay, sweetie?"

I snatched the water, some of it splashed out of the glass onto my lap.

"I'm fine," I said through clenched teeth, not even bothering to wipe the spilled water. He was lucky that my mouth was dry like the Sahara desert and my tongue felt like wool. That was the only thing that kept me from going off at that moment. All I could do at that point was down the entire glass of water.

"Mimi, I know this is a shock. I told you that I would be back for you," he said with a shrug. I guess that was supposed to make things between us better.

I slammed the glass onto the table, upset that he thought that he could just barge in after all of this time and say something as simple as that.

"Thanks for fulfilling your promise, like ten years later. I really appreciate it," I said dryly.

"Mia, give your dad a chance," Aunt Lena pleaded. She kissed me on the cheek and left the room. I was happy that at least for the moment, she was calm and she was not going to knock me into next Sunday.

"Look Mia, I can explain," my dad said as he took a seat across from me at the dining room table.

"Baby girl, I know I messed things up between us. I just couldn't live like we were. I'm sure that you remember that your mother was not always in her right mind. I begged her to get some help when she got worse and she flat-out refused. She knew deep down that she needed it, but she just stayed in denial about her mental health issues.

"It was driving us apart. It's hard to rationalize with a person who doesn't see things rationally. I don't know if you even knew that your mother was hospitalized for a month after you were born. At first, we thought that it was just general post- partum depression. The doctor diagnosed her as being bipolar. He said that she would continue to have these things called manic episodes, meaning that sometimes she would be irritable and act out in different ways that may be harmful to herself and others around her. He also said that there might be times when she was extremely depressed. He described it as either she would be extremely up or extremely down." I listened as he rambled off all of the information that I wished I had known a long time ago.

"The doctor made her behavior make more sense. Your mom had been like that since I met her. That didn't stop me from loving her though. When she went on the medication, things got so much better for us. She could concentrate in school, and her moods weren't so extreme.

"When you were about six or seven, I found out that your mother stopped taking her medication. She said that she didn't need it anymore. That she felt better and she was cured. That wasn't true. I tried to convince her to take her medication and she refused. She started to deny that she ever had a problem. Then she started accusing me of things that I didn't do. It became harder to be with her. I had to make a decision on how I wanted to live my life, because I couldn't stay around with things the way they were. I knew that the situation was not healthy for any of us."

"So you left?" I interrupted. I was in tears by this. "I can see why you left Mama, by why me?" I said as I slammed my hand on the table.

"I made sure that you were taken care of Mia. I stayed with my mother until I found a good job. I continued to pay for the house and I took the money left to me by my grandfather when he died and paid the house off. I wanted to make sure that you would have a roof over your head no matter what. I also set up a bank account that your mother had complete access to so that I could put money in it to pay for whatever you needed. I put extra in on birthdays and holidays and for anything that you would need around the beginning of the school year."

"Wait, you mean Mama knew where you were the entire time!"

"No, she didn't," my dad answered. "I eventually moved out of my mother's house into my own home. Patrice didn't know where I was. Once she found out that I was coming over here to see you at Lena's she threatened to get a restraining order on me. She told me that I had to stay away or else she would call the police on me and tell them that I was beating her up. Mia, I was trying to start a career in law, and I didn't need that. So I did what she asked, while still maintaining the bills and financial care for you."

I watched as my father told the story of our lives. As I looked into his face, I saw how handsome he still was. He still kept his dark, wavy hair cut close and his mocha colored skin was still smooth and flawless. The past few years had been kind to him, more so than they had been to my mother. They were only in their late thirties.

"So now I'm supposed to believe that you're back for good? That you aren't going anywhere? You can see how hard it would be for me after your track record, can't you?" I was trying to absorb this whole moment as best I could.

"Mia, I know that I deserve that. But I want you to understand that I was always going to follow through on my promise to come back to you. I hate the way that things went down, but at the time, I didn't see any other way to solve the problem. I had worked so hard to get through school to fulfill my dreams. Patrice did too. We were supposed to take the Bar Exam together. We had dreams to start our own law firm. But I soon saw that it was not going to be something that could happen. Your mom was not capable of doing that at the time. So what was I supposed to do, let my life fall apart too?"

"Fine, Daddy, I can see that. But what about me? I didn't have any mental health problems. Do you realize that you left me too? And what about your family? I guess they took sides without even really knowing what was going on in our household because you were their blood. But I'm your blood too!

"I still can't figure out how things could go from seeing my uncle and aunts and grandmother all of the time to an occasional phone call and seeing them at holidays, and even that fell off! I guess they thought that they could replace the value of them spending time with me with all of the bullshit toys and clothes that they bought me! I didn't want all of that shit. I wanted to feel like they loved me no matter what was going on between you and Mama! Do you realize that I started to hate them just as much as I felt that they hated me and my mom?"

By now, we were both crying. I had so much pain built up inside of me that I had to let all of it out.

"I felt like they were mad at Mama, so they took it out on me! They let it be all about them and their feelings on the situation and not about what I needed. I was innocent in the whole situation and they didn't care! I mean, I needed them too! I missed them too! Didn't they care that I was having trouble with the fact that my father left us!

"Things got to the point where their phone calls and visits felt like they thought that they were obligated to do that. I know I was kind of young, but I felt it. I *felt* how they were mad at Mama for the way that she was acting. I felt like they blamed the whole break up on her. They seemed so fake when they came by and called. It made me wonder if they ever really cared for Mama and me. You know, all of the visits and calls finally stopped after you left for good and I was glad that they did. I didn't want to be bothered with anyone who didn't really want to be bothered with me!" I was rambling on, but I had to get it all off of my chest, off my heart, and out of my mind.

"I was so thankful that we had Mookie and Aunt Lena," I continued. "I couldn't believe that your family just stopped coming around and calling the way they did, because of all of the things between you and Mama. I decided that if that was what being a family meant to your relatives, I didn't want to be a family with them anyway!"

By now, he wasn't even looking me in the eye. My dad just sat at the table and twiddled his thumbs nervously as I hurled all my hurt and anger at him. I had waited a long time to get all of that out of my system. I felt better, but I was still hurting.

"Mia, all I can say is that I am truly sorry. I prayed every night that you could forgive me for my decisions and that you could understand what I felt I had to do. I'm not asking you to agree with my decision, but just understand that I did the best that I could do at the time. I know that we can't get that time back or make up for any thing that we lost, but we can start over from here.

"And, as for my family, I apologize for them too. I tried to encourage them to stay in your life, but for whatever reason, they chose to handle things the way that they did. I'm not proud of it. I can't make excuses for it. I wished that they could have been more mature about the situation and that they would have realized that the things that were going on were strictly between me and Patrice and it was none of their business. But I guess their true colors and character showed through and if you can't forgive them then I can see why. I'm not going to ask you to forgive them. They were wrong in the way that they treated you and Patrice. I was wrong for not being firmer in encouraging them to go and spend more time with you. I am guilty of that myself. All I can do now is just pick up with you from here and hope that you will accept me back in your life."

He stared at me intently. I stared back, trying to search his eyes and see if he was being sincere. I was so torn because part of me wanted to tell him: 'Fuck you, go on with the rest of your life!' The other part of me wanted to embrace him and feel like his little girl again.

"I don't know," I said. "I need a little time. This is all too quick."

"I understand, Mimi. Look, here is all of my contact information. Call me when you are ready and we can start out slow. Like maybe having lunch or something. I don't want to push you, but I'm letting you know that I'm never leaving again. I will be by here again if you don't call me in a couple days. I'm not going to lose you, Mia. Not again. I'm not going anywhere."

I looked at him as he wrote down about six numbers and an email address on a piece of paper. I guess he was serious about all of this.

"I'll leave now. And tell your Aunt Lena I said thanks and to keep in touch." He got up from the table and stopped as he was walking by me. He bent down and kissed me on the cheek.

"Mia, you are my baby girl and I love you. Just because I left didn't mean that I ever stopped loving you. I'll always be your Daddy, just like I promised. I look forward to your call." And at that, he left.

I couldn't stop the tears flowing. I just sat at the table and released all the years of pain and loneliness through the tears that ran down my face. I couldn't believe that he had actually come back for me. Did that count for something? I thought about the charm bracelet that he gave me and how I had taken it off what seemed like so long ago. I thought about how that bracelet symbolized his promises of love and protection and how I had taken it off and started to live my life void of the feeling that he would ever be there for me again.

I touched the spot on my cheek where my dad had kissed me. I smiled at the fact that his kiss still made me feel like his little girl. The little girl who was the object of her father's affection. The little girl who was absolutely adored by her father. This time as I cried when he left, I didn't feel abandoned. I knew he would be back.

Chapter 11

I DECIDED TO GIVE MY DAD A CHANCE. I GOT DOWN ON MY KNEES AND prayed that things would be different this time. I honestly felt in my heart that they would. And he kept his word, he came by Aunt Lena's everyday to check on me. It became easier for us to talk and I began feeling more secure about out relationship.

I even told my mother that he had come back in my life. Well, actually Aunt Lena told her and my mother asked me what I thought about it. I told her that I was happy that he had come back. I also told her that I wanted her to take the time that she needed to get better. It was like ever since my dad came back around, I had this feeling that things could be right in my life again. I was amazed that she was okay with all of it. She said that letting go of the bitterness and pain that she had been holding on to was part of her recovery process.

After my first reunion with my dad, I have to admit, I still felt bitter.

All of these questions just kept going through my mind. Why did he leave? How could you just walk away from your child? Did he even really care? What made him come back now?

Mookie put an end to those questions for me.

"Mimi, don't be so selfish," he told me as we talked on the ride to school.

"Me? You think I'm being selfish?" I couldn't believe him. Didn't he know that I was the victim in this whole situation?

"Yeah," he continued. "I would do anything, and I mean *anything* for my dad to walk through our front door this evening. But that's not going to happen! But yours did.

"Just because he's your dad doesn't mean that he's not capable of making mistakes. He made one. Hell, a big one. But he's here now, putting all of the cards on the table. No bluffing. No bullshitting. I'm not saying that you don't tell him how you feel and that you should act like things are all cool between you two because they aren't. But you can't change the past. You should tell him that you want him around, which I know you do. If you do that, don't waste your time trying to make him pay for his past mistakes. Or you can tell him to get the hell on and in that case, don't cry about it if he really does leave. It's your choice to make. But I think he's for real. Give him a chance."

I looked at Mookie and I swear for a minute, I saw a tear quickly roll down his face. I guess the point he made helped to put some things in perspective for me. His advice sounded so prophetic. It *was* my decision to make. And I did want my father in my life.

So I made that happen.

My dad and I talked everyday, mostly about school, but about all kinds of things. He was interested in what I wanted to do with my life. I don't really remember anybody asking me that besides an occasional school counselor. I had never really though about it before.

My dad came and took me out to lunch one Saturday afternoon. He pulled up in a candy apple red 600 CL Benz. I couldn't believe his ride! I went out to the car and walked around it as I checked it out.

The candy apple color was so sweet that it made me want to taste it. The rims were so shiny that I checked out my reflection in them just to give myself a once over before we left. For the first time, I wondered what my dad did for a living. I knew it had to be something in law, but I wasn't sure exactly what. It occurred to me that I had never asked him up until now. I made a mental note to ask over lunch.

We drove to downtown Atlanta. As we cruised down Peachtree, he asked me where I wanted to eat. There were too many choices, so I decided to eat somewhere that I had never eaten before. The car skated down the street and we turned into the parking lot for the Cheesecake Factory just as I had gotten used to the admiring stares of people wondering who were the superstars riding in the car.

"You sure this is where you want to eat?" my dad asked. "We can go wherever you want to go."

"This is it. I've never been here before." I had heard about the restaurant but had never been to it. It was a warm October afternoon and I saw the people eating outside on the patio.

"Daddy, why don't we get a seat on the patio?"

"Okay, Mimi." He asked the hostess for a table for two on the patio. Fortunately, we didn't have to wait because a table was already available.

The hostess led us to the table. Daddy pulled the chair out for me to sit down. I smiled because he hadn't lost his touch. He always had this way of making me feel like a princess. The hostess left us with menus and told us that our waitress would be along shortly. We decided on our orders just as the waitress came to ask us what we wanted to drink. We also ordered appetizers and our entrée.

I watched as the cars crept up and down Peachtree in Saturday afternoon traffic.

"You enjoying yourself?" Daddy asked as he sipped his water with lemon.

"I am. Thanks."

We continued with our conversation and the food finally arrived.

"Hey, Mimi. I was thinking that maybe you could come over to the house and meet the family soon. I mean, if you're ready."

I played with my food as I thought about what he was asking me. I was enjoying having him all to myself, but I knew realistically, he did have another family.

"Sure. When?"

"I was thinking maybe next weekend. It's supposed to be nice weather and we could cookout and have a last dip in the pool before it gets cool for the winter. How does that sound?"

How do you say, '*I could really give a damn about meeting your family. The family that you took care of instead of being with my mom and me. I don't really give a rat's ass about meeting the woman that you married instead of my mama*'?

All that came out was, "That sounds great, Daddy."

Then I added, "Can Mookie come too?" I needed reinforcements. I didn't want to be anywhere that I would be uncomfortable.

"Yeah, that would be great. I would love to have my nephew come over. He's always welcome. I guess the two of you are close, huh?"

"The closest. He's more like a brother. Mama and Aunt Lena made sure of it."

There was a silence as we ate.

"Daddy, I never asked you what you do for a living." *Yeah, what's got you driving a big car, dressing in expensive clothes, and paying for your own life and my life too?*

"Oh, I'm District Attorney for Fulton County," he answered casually.

"Hmm, cool." I breathed a slight sigh of relief that it was something legal. I don't know why I thought that it would be anything but a legal gig. I guess being a lawyer is as legal as it gets.

We ordered cheesecake, laughed and talked some more. Women walked by and I caught them staring at my dad. He noticed them too and I saw him snicker. He still had it. As I looked at him, I noticed that he reminded me of the banker that Stony fell in love with in that movie 'Set it off'.

After we ate, we rode around downtown for a while. We stopped off at Lenox Mall and he took me shopping. I couldn't believe that I had spent an entire day with my dad. And the best part was, that things were cool between us.

I couldn't help but think that something had to go wrong. Things were going too well. The conversation I had with Mookie popped back into my mind. I had the ball in my court and I was going to make things happen. I was going to make sure that I tried to have a decent relationship with my dad. For Mookie's sake. Hell, for my sake. God knows that after all of the hell that I had been through, I deserved it.

Chapter 12

THE FOLLOWING SATURDAY, MOOKIE AND I GOT DRESSED AND LEFT TO go to my dad's for a cookout. No, I wasn't trying to play myself. I knew that it was more than just a cookout. I was going to meet *the family.*

I spent the entire week imagining what they looked like, how they would act. At first, I imagined his wife as a cute little homemaker who would come to the door to greet me with a plate of fresh baked cookies wearing a white button down shirt, a full knee length skirt, with pearls around her neck and her hair pulled back in a bun. Like the nice little housewives you see on television. What the hell? I know nobody was like that anymore. At least not where I'm from.

Then I imagined her as the Cruella DeVille type. You know the bitchy chick from the Dalmatians movie. I imagined her standing there to greet me as the gust of autumn wind blew the door open. She would be dressed in a body-hugging black dress with long black gloves that climbed up her arms. Her long, black hair would hang down her shoulders as she puffed on a cigarette in one of those long holders, like the ladies in those old 1930s movies. She would be like the 'Mommy Dearest' type. Sweet to you in public, but in private she would be the evil step-mother barking commands as I scrubbed floors and she screamed about wire hangers.

I had no clue who this chick would be. And to boot, my father had a daughter that, he said, was two years younger than me. So that meant that when he left us, he started another family soon after.

I had a sister. A half-sister. I wondered if she looked anything like me. Although I looked like my mother and my aunt, I did have my dad's thick eyebrows and his thick wavy hair.

Mookie pulled up in front of what looked like a mansion. We were in a neighborhood over off Riverside Drive in Alpharetta that we never knew existed.

Damn! My dad was living like a king. The slate colored, Spanish styled, stucco house sat back off the street on at least a thousand acres of land. Okay, I'm exaggerating about the land, but damn, it was a lot of land! A security gate kept unwanted guests off the property.

We buzzed the house at the gate and a woman's voice answered. She buzzed the gate and let us in when we identified ourselves.

We drove for what seemed like days down the winding driveway. The grounds were neatly manicured and all types of brightly colored flowers popped out through the rich green of the grounds.

"What the fuck, Mimi! What the hell does Uncle Cliff do for a living?"

"Oh, he's the District Attorney for Fulton County," I said, as casually as my dad had answered me when I asked the same question.

"Yeah, well, this shit is ridiculous! Do you see this?"

"Yeah, I see it all right," I responded. I sat back in my seat and admired how my dad was living. It's not like my life was all that bad, but I wondered if things would have been different in my life if this had been my home. Just looking at the house explained how he was able to afford paying for me and my mom and his own family.

"Damn, Mimi. I'm sorry."

I looked over at Mookie.

"For what?"

"Does all of this make you feel cheated?"

I couldn't lie. I felt a twinge of jealousy when we drove up. He had been living like this and I had, well, I had been living.

"No," I lied. "Don't forget, he's my dad. I think that I'm entitled to all of this too."

Mookie laughed. "Hell, yeah cuz! You got that right."

As we got out of the car, my dad ran up to us. He was dressed casually in a pair of jean shorts and a polo t- shirt with an apron that read 'Kiss the Cook'.

"Hey ya'll!' he said, as he ran over and hugged us.

"I'm so glad you came. Mookie, it's good to see you. You're so grown up now."

"It's good to see you too, Uncle Cliff. It's been a while. Doesn't look like you're doing too bad over here though."

My dad just laughed off Mookie's comment.

"Follow me. The food is already on the grill. I'll show you where to get changed. I hope you brought your bathing suits."

We grabbed our bags from Mookie's car and followed my dad into the house. My mouth was so wide open; I could have trapped flies in it. My eyes jumped around the room from the marble floors and high ceilings with gold chandeliers in the foyer to the winding staircase in front of me. Pictures from all of those dead, important artists that you learn about in school, hung on the walls.

We followed Daddy through the house toward the back patio. I took in as much of the rooms that we passed through as I could. I knew from that point on that I could get used to making all of this mine too.

We walked through the French doors out into the backyard. Or should I say the desert oasis. Ahead of us was a pool with Jacuzzi. There were large rocks with clear water poring off of them into a pool with a crystal blue bottom. There was a large patio with a lounging and dining area. He had a damn kitchen in his backyard!

"Hey, you two can change in the pool house. And make yourselves comfortable; you're at home."

He pointed to the small house that sat to the left in the corner of the yard. We ran off toward the house with our bags. While we changed, Mookie looked at me and his eyes said what I was thinking. *What the hell?* My dad was living like a king.

When we came outside, my dad was on the grill flipping burgers. He motioned for us to take a dip in the pool while we waited for the food. The warm water invited me in and soon Mookie was off doing laps in the pool. I sat casually halfway in the water soaking in the sun. You know how us girls do it; cute suit, cute hair. Just too damn cute to get wet.

"Hey, there you two are!" I turned at the sound of my dad's voice. Two females came out of the French doors. The older one was carrying another tray of food for the grill. The younger one was walking my way.

They were both light-skinned and I had to admit to myself, very pretty. Cruella DeVille had on a pair of light blue capris, a matching tank top and a pair of heeled gold sandals. She had on so much jewelry that it made me glad that I had on my shades. My dad said something to her as he worked the grill. I saw her cut her eyes over at me.

In the meanwhile, the younger Ms. Priss sashayed right over and sat at the edge of the pool next to me. She suddenly embraced me.

"I'm so glad to meet you!" she exclaimed, as she hugged me so tight that I thought I would stop breathing right there.

"I'm Janaya. You must be Mia! I'm so glad to meet you!"

I would have answered her if I could breathe. As she continued to hug me, Cruella glided over to us at the pool.

"Janaya, give the girl some room," she said in a smooth voice. "I'm Genise," she said, as she coldly extended her hand for me to shake. I knew I wasn't going to get a great, big hug like Janaya gave me, but I expected her to at least act like she was happy to meet me. I was starting to think that she might live up to the nickname I gave her.

Janaya backed off, still smiling this silly smile as I took my hand, still wet from my sitting in the pool, and reached to shake Genise's. She pulled back politely, taking a napkin to wipe her wet hand as her face twisted in a nice/nasty look.

I looked at her with eyebrows raised. *Oh, this heifer just tried me!* I think that she noticed my reaction to her actions and her twisted face quickly turned into a smile. The kind that the beauty queens wear. You know, the fake ones that didn't really tell you much about the way the person felt except that they were being phony as hell.

"Nice to meet you, Genise," I said, accentuating her name just a bit. Just enough to let her know that I peeped her game.

"Well, you and your cousin - Uh, what's his name?"

"*Family* calls him Mookie, but you would probably prefer to call him by his name, Michael," I said sarcastically.

"Oh yes, Michael. You two enjoy yourselves and make yourselves at home." Her offer sounded like she had practiced it over and over in an attempt to make it sound as sincere as possible. She quickly walked away as if she was glad to be finished with the chore of introducing herself to me. I turned around to see Janaya still looking at me.

"What?" I asked. Why the hell was she all in my grill like this? I wasn't used to little sisters.

"You have to excuse my mother. She has trouble speaking to people because she has a stick up her ass most of the time." We both burst out laughing.

"Wow, we both have the same eyebrows. And the wavy dark hair," Janaya remarked.

I looked at her through my shades and realized that she was right. We did have those things in common.

We sat and talked the rest of the afternoon over burgers and barbequed chicken, pasta salad, and lemonade. I found out that Janaya was actually okay. She was a lot better that her bitchy mother. Genise stayed away and busied herself with cooking and cleaning. She ran around like a chicken with her head cut off and in between that, she would find ways to wrap herself territorially around my father. I wanted to tell her that he was my father, so I wasn't trying to sleep with her man.

I was glad that I hadn't tricked myself into thinking that my father's wife would be anything other than the bitch that she was. Janaya, on the other hand, was a pleasant surprise.

Mookie and I went home with full stomachs, happy to have a change of scenery for a while. When we pulled up, I saw my girlfriend Keyshawna drive up in an old school ride. She sat in front of the house in a '96 Impala, black on 22 inch Buttnicks. Even Mookie had to take a second look at the ride.

Keyshawna was one of my girlfriends from school. Not that she actually went to school. We met when we were about elementary school aged. She grew up down the block from my aunt with her three brothers who never worked unless the job was illegal. Her mother died when she was young and she was raised by her thugged out brothers and her workaholic father.

Keyshawna had potential to do well. She was a very intelligent girl. But she had an affinity for the things that would keep her in trouble. I liked hanging with her because she was crazy and there was never a dull moment.

"Girl, where you been?" she yelled from the car.

"Long story. Wait up," I said. I ran into the house and put my things down in my room. I told Mookie to tell Aunt Lena that I would be back later. I knew that he didn't like me to hang out with Keyshawna, but he let it go that time because he wanted to get to Tony's studio that evening to lay down some tracks.

I ran back outside and jumped into the car with Keyshawna. We rode off rolling down Redan Road, turning onto South Hairston Road.

"Damn, girl, where you get this ride from?" I asked as I admired the cream and wood-grain interior.

"You know how my brother, Kevin, do it. He let me get the ride to take it for a spin."

"Man, this thing is tight!" I said.

"Yeah, it is, isn't it? Wanna hit South Dekalb Mall?" she suggested.

"Sure," I agreed.

We rode down the street as I told her what had gone on earlier that day at my dad's.

The T.I. CD was playing as we cruised down the street. We chilled out because anyone that lived in Dekalb County Georgia knew that the police were always on everybody's ass. Today, the motorcycle cop was on ours.

"You got your license on you, don't you, girl?" I asked. It was not too much to ask her a question like that. I told you that she was a wild chick.

"Of course, just play it cool. You know how I hate the Po- Po's."

I sat back in my seat as Keyshawna pulled over to the curb. The cop pulled over behind us.

I watched him get off his bike and walk over to the driver's side of the car.

"Can I see your license and registration please?" He looked at us funny as he asked the question. I knew he was wondering our age. Keyshawna showed him all of the ID and information he asked for.

"Ma'am is this your car?"

"Yes, why do you ask?" she asked calmly.

"Ma'am, please step out of the car."

Bam! There it is. You know that you're in deep shit if they ask you to step out of the car.

"Ma'am, this car is stolen," he said. as he put cuffs on my home girl. "You are under arrest for possession of a stolen vehicle."

I sat back in the car as my heart almost beat right out of my chest. *What the fuck!*

After the officer had handcuffed Keyshawna, he came around to the passenger side and asked me to get out of the car. Before I knew it, I was handcuffed and we were both sitting on the curb as he radioed in for back up.

"What the fuck, Keyshawna? A stolen car?"

"Damn, Mia, shut the fuck up and sit tight! We cool. When we get to jail, I'll call my brother and his lawyer will get us off. Especially you 'cause you ain't never been to jail before."

Jail! Jail! Did she just say jail?

"Damn right I ain't ever been to jail before! I don't do that shit!"

As we sat arguing, the cop came around the car with a bag of something white. Oh shit! Drugs too? I thought that I was going to piss on myself.

"I don't suppose that one of you will own up to this either?" the cop asked.

Just as I was about to pass out, I heard Keyshawna say, "It's hers officer."

This bitch was lucky that I was handcuffed. That didn't stop me from trying to dig into her ass.

"You lying bitch! You know that shit isn't mine! You know I don't know nothin' about any of this shit! Tell him!"

Keyshawna just sat on the curb next to me, expressionless. She didn't even try to take the rap. Two patrol cars pulled up and we were both escorted to a car. I was going to jail for some shit that I didn't do. Aunt Lena was going to kill me. I just knew it. I could kick myself. Why did I get in the car with that crazy bitch, Keyshawna, anyway? I did and now I was on my way to jail. Shit!

As I sat in the back of the patrol car, I looked over at Keyshawna in the back of the other car. She stared at me and mouthed words telling me to keep my mouth shut. Hell, I didn't really know what to say anyway. Getting arrested was not my thing. I was at a loss for words. I was between breaking down in tears and being ready to get out of this car and beat Keyshawna's ass for not letting me know that the stolen car we were riding in had drugs in it.

I should have known better than to fuck with that messy bitch. What the hell was I thinking? I had such a decent day. But I knew that things wouldn't always stay good. I just had to think of a way to explain this to my aunt. I think I was more scared of her than of going to jail.

Go to jail! Go to jail! The words just kept replaying in my head.

I knew one thing. They had better not put me in the same cell as Keyshawna when we got there. If they did, I would be catching whatever the official charge was for whipping her ass to the point of unconsciousness. At least then, I would be in jail for something that I really and truly did.

What the hell had I gotten myself into?

Chapter 13

I'M NOT SURE HOW PEOPLE GET USED TO BEING IN JAIL. I KNEW immediately that it wasn't for me. They took Keyshawna and me to Dekalb County YDC- the youth detention center. Fortunately, I didn't have to deal with Keyshawna when we got there. They ended up transferring her downtown to the Regional Youth Detention Center. I was happy because I knew I needed to get my ass out of here and if she was in with me, I was going to catch an assault charge that night.

I stayed there for two days and it was absolute hell. The orange jumpsuit, the slippers, the girls that tried me. I mean, everyone in there thought that they were gay. Maybe they had been there too long. I stayed to myself, but did talk to a few people. Just to make it seem like I wasn't stuck up or anything. Actually, it was crazy because I saw a lot of people I knew. People that I had wondered what kind of hand life had dealt them. Come to find out they were in jail.

My court date came up on Monday and I was happy for that. I knew Aunt Lena and Mookie would be there. I got a phone call through to her and she was so upset that she passed the phone to Mookie and refused to speak to me. He told me that both of them would be there in court, but that I had to give Aunt Lena time to calm herself, because she was beyond pissed off.

On Monday morning at 10 a.m. the officer brought me into juvenile court in handcuffs. I heard a muffled cry that turned into a loud wail. I turned to see Aunt Lena in tears. Mookie rubbed her back to calm her and winked at me reassuringly. Seeing her so upset at what I had gotten myself into brought tears to my own eyes.

They had gotten an attorney for me named Terry Walters. She was an intelligent, young attorney who also happened to be fly as hell.

The officer took the cuffs off my wrists after he brought me in, but the shackles remained on my ankles.

Ms. Walters spoke to me briefly before the judge came back into the courtroom and told me to keep quiet and let her do her job. I should only speak when spoken to.

Fine with me.

The judge came in and everyone rose to his or her feet. The bailiff told everyone to be seated and our name was called on the docket.

The judge began reading the charges. They were basically charging me for being and accessory to stealing the vehicle and possession of the drugs. I tried to stop crying, but hearing the charges brought this all too close to home.

"Young lady, why are you crying?" the judge asked.

I looked at Ms. Walters who nodded her head in agreement for me to answer the question.

"Your Honor, I've never been in trouble before. I did not do what I am being charged with. I admit that I was with the wrong person and that I should not have been hanging out with her. I got caught up and I would take it all back if I could. I apologize."

She looked down at me over her glasses, glanced at some papers, and then back at me.

"Ms. Lawson, I see that you have no previous record. I understand that the young lady that you were with has an extensive one. I also understand that she was in court this morning and that she took responsibility for her actions in the hope that you could be cleared. Ms. Lawson, you cannot take your actions back. What's done is done. I only hope that in the future, you use your intelligence to keep better, more positive people in your company."

I nodded my head as I sniffled. The tears were still rolling. I couldn't believe that Keyshawna had done the right thing.

"I hope that the few days you spent in jail will be more than enough to encourage you that this is not the life that you would like to lead. . Now, Ms. Walters, is the parent or guardian for this child present?"

"Yes, Your Honor-,"

Before she could finish speaking, Ms. Walters was interrupted. The courtroom turned to look toward the interjecting voice.

"Your Honor, I am Ms. Lawson's parent. I am her father, Clifton Lawson."

"Well, well, Mr. Lawson, it's good to see you," the judge said as my dad stepped up from the crowd.

"May I approach the bench?" he asked.

"Yes, please," she answered.

They talked for a minute and I looked at Ms. Walters. She winked at me. I wondered if she knew this all along. I looked back at Aunt Lena. She just smiled and nodded.

"Ms. Lawson, you have previously been in temporary custody of your aunt Lena Reed. You will now be released into your father's custody. And Ms. Lawson?"

"Yes, Your Honor?"

"I expect that this is the last time that I will see you in my courtroom. It seems that you have a strong support system. Many of the children that I see have absolutely no one to support them, whether it is financially or emotionally. That is not true in your case. I wish you a happy life, free of the legal system. Case dismissed. Bailiff, Ms. Lawson should now be remanded in custody of her father, Clifton Lawson. Next case."

The bailiff came over and opened the lock on the shackles.

"Is that it?" I asked Ms. Walters.

"That's it, honey!" she said, as she packed up some papers in her suitcase. "Oh, and luckily, your aunt told me who your dad was. I knew him and was able to get in touch with him. You are one fortunate girl. Do me a favor and stay out of trouble. All of this," she said waving her hand around the courtroom, "is definitely not your style."

She walked away as my family came up to me.

"I'm still kicking you ass!" Aunt Lena said as she half laughed, half cried. She grabbed me and hugged me tight, as we all left the courtroom.

"Cuz, I owe you an ass kickin' too," Mookie said, punching my shoulder. "But I'll save it for later."

"Mia, you ready? We have some paperwork to finish and I have to take you to get your personals released."

I looked at Aunt Lena.

"Mimi, I think it will be good for you to live with Cliff for a while. I mean, he's back in your life and you two deserve a chance. But, you know I'm not going anywhere. I'm still Auntie and my house is your house."

I understood what she was saying. I was mad for a second. They had made this decision without asking me. But I guess I left myself little room to make decisions on my own after what I had just put them all through.

"It's cool Aunt Lena, I understand. I messed up big, and I'm so sorry. I'm just glad that Keyshawna owned up to all of this."

"Yeah, well, she'll be in lockup for a minute," my dad said.

We went to get my personal items and I was too happy to be free. I had never appreciated my freedom until it was taken from me and now I was allowed to have it back.

My dad took me past Aunt Lena's and I packed my things.

"Lena, I'll bring her back for the weekends. You and Mookie know that you two are always welcome to come out to see her at anytime. You don't need an invitation."

I waved goodbye to my aunt and my cousin. I caught myself getting ready to cry. They had been the only family that I had known for the past few years. But why was I trippin'? They weren't going anywhere. I thought about that big ass house that I would be living in. What could be better?

We rode silently for a while, and then my dad told me that he would be transferring me to a high school in Alpharetta that week. He said that he also had a bedroom set up for me.

"I hope that you like it. If you don't, you can change it to suit your own taste when you get settled. I really hope that you will make yourself comfortable. You will be at home. Plus, Janaya is too happy that you are coming to live with us," he said smiling.

Hmph, no mention of how my lovely step- mother was happy for me to be coming.

"What about your wife?"

"What about her?" he said, as we pulled into the driveway.

"Is she happy too, that I'm coming to stay?"

"Yeah, why would you ask that? Genise is thrilled that you are coming. She thought that you were so beautiful when you came by for the cookout."

Funny, I didn't get that feeling.

"What should I call her?"

" 'Genise' will be fine. Come on. Let me get your things."

We grabbed my bags from the trunk of the car and went in the house. He led me to my room.

"You and Janaya will be on this side of the house. You two can make as much noise over here as you want to. You have your own phone line over here that the two of you will share. You will also share the bathroom over here."

My room was ridiculous. It was like the size of my aunt's living room, dining room, and kitchen combined. It was decorated in pink, of course, my favorite color. I had my own television and stereo. There was a full sized, mahogany wood, sleigh bed decorated with a pink comforter and lots of accented throw pillows.

As soon as he left me to get settled, there was a knock at the door.

"Come in."

"Hey, sis!"

It was Janaya.

"Hey, yourself," I said as I put clothes in my dresser drawers.

"So, I hope you like the room. They let me decorate it. I thought that it looked like you."

"You did a good job. Thanks."

"Girl, put that stuff down. You have plenty of time to get all of that together. Let me show you around," Janaya said pulling me by my hand.

"Okay." Somehow I didn't think that I had a choice. Besides, I needed to see all of the rest of this mansion that I was going to live in.

She was showing me her room as the phone rang. Her room was decorated in pastels and looked feminine just like mine. I had to admit that she did have good taste.

"No, I can't come tonight girl….I told you that my sister was moving in…Man, forget him! Anyway, I have to go. I'm helping my sister get comfortable in our house…Yeah, I'll do the party this weekend. Okay, later."

I acted as if I wasn't listening to her. Instead I occupied myself browsing the pictures that she had of herself and some friends on her dresser.

"I know you heard the conversation. I hope that just because you got locked up this one time you're not going to let that spoil the fun. I heard that you been out there in the streets for a while. Me and you could have some real fun," she said, with a sly grin on her face.

I just looked at her like she was crazy. Well, well, well. What was this? Daddy's little angel. Spoiled. little, rich girl. I had a feeling that this chick was a little more off the chain than I could be.

Chapter 14

I SAT IN THE DEN LOOKING AT MY PHOTO ALBUMS. I LOOKED AT THE smiling faces, people hugging, people dancing, wondering where all of that went.

When did it all stop? Where were those people in the pictures who were so happy? There had been so many twists and turns lately and life had me going along for the ride, though I felt more like a passenger than the driver.

Why did Janaya get the opportunity to live in a house with both of her parents, who were married to each other? Why didn't I get the opportunity to have my parents be together like that?

I was happy that my dad came back into my life, but what was wrong with us that he, my mom, and I couldn't be the happy family that we always wanted to be?

I sat on that couch for a moment trying to figure it out. The only conclusion that I came to was that it just wasn't meant to be, for whatever reason. I was used to taking what life dealt to me, but now I was ready to get in the driver's seat. Both of my parents were good people, but they had their own demons and issues to fight. I made a promise to myself at that point to always look out for number one - Mia.

I would be starting school next week and my new school was not something I was really looking forward to. It was the second school I would attend in my junior year. Keeping up my grades was one of my major concerns. My dad was sending me to one of those white schools in Alpharetta. Okay, so it was probably not all white, but I could guarantee there would be more white people there than at my school in Stone Mountain.

Janaya was excited that I would be starting school with her and she had already started a buzz about "The New Girl" coming.

I called Aunt Lena and Mookie everyday. It was hard enough adjusting to living in a new house and besides that I had to get to know my dad all over again, along with getting to know Janaya and Genise.

Janaya was not a problem. She could be a bit much, but she was sweet and I could tell that she was genuinely happy to have me there. Genise was another story. I knew that no matter how hard she tried to hide it, she didn't like me or the fact that I was living there. We just tolerated each other. Our conversations were brief and were never really about anything.

The Lawsons ate dinner together every night. At first, I wanted to gag, but I got used to the idea of coming together as a family each night and decided that it wasn't all that bad.

"So, Mimi, you excited about starting school Monday?" Daddy asked.

"I am. At first, I wasn't, but it'll be a fresh start for me," I said as I played with my mashed potatoes.

I forgot to mention that Genise was not a good cook. No matter what she cooked, it was disgusting. About the only thing that tasted right was the sweet tea.

"Dad, I was thinking that maybe Mia should get her license," Janaya said.

I shot an icy stare at her. I had been thinking about getting my license and had asked her if she thought that my dad would let me, but I wanted to bring it up to him on my own, not at the dinner table in front of Cruella DeVille. I couldn't believe that Janaya put me on blast like that.

There was complete silence at first. Then my dad spoke. "Actually, that doesn't sound like a bad idea," he said, as he nodded in agreement.

Genise's face tightened in disapproval. "But, Cliff, she probably doesn't even have a permit," she said, politely trying to make excuses.

"Sure I do. I've been driving on it for the past 6 months. I took driver's ed already and I'm actually a pretty good driver. I just haven't gotten my license yet," I said in response. There! Busted her bubble.

"Great Mimi! That means that you and I have a date at the DMV tomorrow morning so that you can get your license. Then you can drive yourself and Janaya to and from school and other school activities," Dad said as he pushed away his plate. I noticed that he had been playing with his food, too. I knew for sure that he hadn't married Genise for her cooking or her polite disposition.

"All right!" Janaya responded. I could see the wheels spinning in her head about all of the places that I could drive her. Genise, on the other hand, had a facial expression like she had just sucked on sour lemons.

"Thanks, Daddy!" I said to him, but staring at Genise. She rolled her eyes and excused herself from the table.

And the winner is, Mia!

I could try to be cool with Genise, but what was the point. I couldn't fake my dislike for her, and something told me that she wouldn't fake hers for me either.

My dad took me to the DMV that Friday and we sat in line all day waiting for my turn. I aced the test, and walked out a licensed driver. He let me drive his Benz home and I thought about how I could get used to driving a luxury car.

He told me that the car that I was to drive was the Toyota Camry parked in the garage. Okay, so it wasn't a Benz, but it was acceptable - air conditioner for the summer, heat for the winter, and a radio and CD player that worked. It was a black, four door and I was happy. You couldn't have paid me a few months ago to think that I would be getting my license, let alone a car.

I called Mookie and told him about it.

"Wow, cuz! And he gave you a car to drive too? You're just livin' it up over there ain't you?"

"Something' like that. I told you that I was going to make the most of this."

We talked for a while and I told him that we would meet up this weekend and that I would come and pick him up for a change.

I chilled out in my room for a while, enjoying my new life. I was living in a luxurious house, I had a car, and my dad was paid. I thought about what my mother was going through. I did want us to be closer and I vowed that no matter what, I would work on having a better relationship with her.

Aunt Lena had given me my mother's address at the halfway house. She could receive mail from people on her contact list as long as they were family members that were encouraging to her rehabilitation.

I sat down and wrote her a letter. It felt good to let all of my feelings out. I just encouraged her to get better and told her not to worry about me. I also told her that I wouldn't mess up again like I did by getting arrested.

I decided to spend a quiet evening in the house. I called Marissa to see what was going on with her. I went to the kitchen to get a snack so that I could go back and chill in my room. I found Genise in the kitchen on the phone.

"I know, Janelle…" she said, talking to her sister. "I hate the way things are now. Cliff didn't even give me any say about bringing Mia in this house. I understand family, but why should I have to deal with his mistakes? I wanted him to run for Circuit Court Judge. How is he going to do that after people get wind that he's brought his little ghetto princess up in my house?…."

Ghetto Princess? It was all that I could do to not confront her. But I decided to stay back behind the kitchen wall and listen to what she really thought of me. I heard her fumbling around in the drawers. I had noticed in the recent weeks that Genise loved to make mixed drinks and she had a thing for Margaritas. The sound of the blender drowned out some of the conversation.

"…Yeah well, he took her to get her license today and gave her one of the cars to drive. And can you believe that he had the nerve to disagree with me about it at dinner the other day?... I know. I hope that she ain't bringin' her ghetto ass up in here thinking' she's going to take over our lives… Her mother? Remember I told you that heifer is in rehab. I heard that she was a real serious user…"

I listened as she tried to sum up my life in one phone call. I could have been heated, but I expected that from her. She acted like I came up in here to take something away from her. Who was she to judge me? She could take her fake attitude and shove it up her ass.

It killed me how she tried to be the proper Ms. Etiquette at her little dinner parties and socials, but I listened to her use slang and incorrect English on the phone with her sister. It made me think that maybe she knew something about being a ghetto princess herself.

I knew one thing, I wasn't about to walk around the house on eggshells because of her stank ass. I barged into the kitchen, interrupting her phone call.

"Well, you know how that goes…" she said as she looked up and saw me entering the kitchen. She continued talking to her sister while changing the conversation as I walked around like I had lived in the house my entire life. I felt her eyes follow me as I gathered my food and reached into the refrigerator to get something to drink.

On the way back to my bedroom, I gave Genise a polite smile. I heard her say something about me making her sick. It was good, because that meant that we were equal in our dislike for one another.

I passed Janaya's room and heard her on the phone, as usual. I sat in my room and ate my snacks as I watched TV until I fell asleep. Janaya woke me up as she busted into my room.

"Mia, get up!" she said, shaking me like she was crazy.

"What the hell do you want?" I said, sitting up straight. "What time is it?"

I looked at the clock and saw that it was after midnight. I looked back at Janaya and saw that she was completely dressed - if you could call what she was wearing dressed.

Janaya was about to be fifteen, but her body said that she was at least twenty-one. The red halter-top that she wore showed all of her D cup breasts and the black pants she had on were so tight, they looked like they were painted on. I looked a little closer and saw that she had plastered on too much makeup. She was too pretty to have on so much.

"Janaya, what the fuck do you have on?"

"Honey, I look good. Anyway, you need to get dressed so we can go," she said, as she checked herself in the mirror.

"Umm, hello! Go where?"

"Mia, too many questions. It's Friday night, we have a car and you have license. Now let's get out of here."

"What about Daddy and your mother? You'll get us in trouble."

She shifted all of her weight onto one leg and stood with her hand on her hip as she sighed. "From what I understand, you didn't have a problem leaving out at night when you lived with your aunt."

"How did you know about that?"

"Don't worry about that," she said, as she pulled me out of the bed. "Mia, don't get over here and act like you didn't run the streets before. I heard about how you were livin' pretty wild while your mother was doin' her thing. We won't get in trouble. They'll never know we're gone. I do this all the time. Difference is now I don't have to have someone come and get me anymore, I got you."

She pushed me toward the bathroom. "Get cleaned up and I'll have your clothes ready. And just to let you know, my parents never pay attention to what I do on this side of the house. They stay on their side and I stay on mine. Daddy's usually too tired after pulling long hours and my mom usually is toasted off playing bartender all night. Now let's go."

I got up to get dressed. I took one more look at Janaya as I walked to the bathroom. I didn't know where we were going, but with the way that she was dressed, I couldn't let her walk out of here alone. At the very least, I would watch out for her tonight while she was doing whatever it was she did.

I realized that this was not the first time that she had alluded to the way that I knew about the streets. I didn't know what she was up to, but I would finally find out tonight. I just hoped that if Janaya found what she was looking for, that she wasn't going to get hurt. I knew that she didn't know as much as she thought she did. Little did I know, Janaya was in a whole world of things that would soon get us into all kinds of trouble.

Chapter 15

I GOT DRESSED AGAINST MY BETTER JUDGMENT. HAVING A CAR TO DRIVE gave us so much freedom. I pulled off of the exit and looking around realized that I wasn't exactly sure where we were. Janaya said that we were somewhere over in Gwinnett County.

As we pulled up in front of the house, Janaya pulled out her cell, calling someone inside to tell him or her to open the door.

The house was *all that*. It sat alone at the end of a cul-de-sac; the first house to be built on that end of the street. Cars were parked all along the curb. It was an exclusive tennis and pool community and I could tell that whoever owned the house had some major cheese.

"Look, when we go in, just chill and don't ask a lot of questions. Just be cool," Janaya said as we approached the door.

"Okay," I agreed. I just wanted to see what it was that she did in her spare time.

We walked around to a door at the back of the house. A girl answered.

"Damn, I was wondering if you would make it Baby Girl! I thought it was going to be just me tonight." The girl looked at me as she spoke to Janaya. She was dressed in even less than Janaya.

"This must be your sister," the girl said as she walked closer to me. She was standing in my face by now, licking her lips.

"Yeah, I'm her sister and I don't go that way," I said quickly, messing up her plans.

"Damn, too bad 'cause you and me could do things," she said as she flicked her tongue ring. "Well, I'm Robin, but when I work my name is Candy. Anyway, Baby Girl," she said turning back to Janaya, "Come on. You look cute tonight." She pulled Janaya by the arm.

"Mia's coming with us," Janaya said, as she grabbed my arm, pulling me along with them.

"Oh, so she's down too?"

"No, not tonight. Maybe later. She's just here to watch," Janaya answered as she winked at me.

The look on my face must have shown my confusion. What the fuck was Janaya doing? We walked through the ridiculously large kitchen, and entered a long hallway that led us to a bedroom. The sounds of men laughing and music booming surrounded us. The smell of weed and food floated through the air. The kitchen counter looked like a mini bar.

Robin opened the door and Janaya ran in behind her. Janaya threw her bag down and started taking things out to prepare for the night. She spoke without looking at me, sensing the disapproving look on my face.

"Chill out, Mia. It'll be fun."

"Fun? Looks like you either strippin' or fuckin' to me," I said, as I stood with my arms crossed. I hated to kill the mood, but I wanted to make sure that she wasn't going to get me mixed up in any bullshit.

"She ain't know?" Robin said as she now stood completely naked in the room. She held her outfit in her hands; a g-string and a string bikini top that left nothing to the imagination.

"No, I didn't tell her Candy. Look, Mia," Janaya said turning to me, "I just do this sometimes. I met Robin a while ago and she put me on to it. I don't work at any clubs or anything because I'm too young. I just do a few parties on the weekends. But you can see for yourself. Just chill with me tonight or you can go home. Robin will bring me home when we're done."

She was crazy if she thought that I was going anywhere. I was already here and no matter how many times Janaya said that she had done this, I wasn't going to leave her here alone.

"Ya'll bitches ready?" Someone peeked in from behind the door of the bedroom just as Janaya finished changing into an outfit as skimpy as Candy's. I had to admit, she looked good in it and I couldn't believe, with all the curves she had that she was only fourteen. I knew the men she was doing a show for wouldn't believe it either; most likely they didn't care.

I turned and looked at the dude who was at the door. He stood in the open doorway, dressed in a throwback jersey, matching hat cocked to the side, jeans, and a pair of tennis shoes that matched his outfit perfectly, looking sexy as hell. He smiled and showed perfect, snow-white teeth.

"Who dat Baby Girl?" he said, nodding toward me.

"Hey, Shawn, this is my sister Mia," she said pulling me toward him. "Take her witchu. We're almost done back here."

"My pleasure," he said, as he grabbed my hand.

"You cool?" I asked over my shoulder.

"I'm fine," Janaya answered. "You go and have fun," she winked as I walked out of the door with Shawn.

As he led me down the hallway, the thump of the bass rattled through my body. We walked into the sunken living room. There was nothing but men and a couple girls sitting on plush couches. One of the chicks was a stud, the other two were feminine, and I swore one of them looked like Mark's friend, Simone. She looked at me as if she recognized me when I first came in, but I turned away just in case it really was her. I didn't really want to have anything to do with her tonight and I had never expected to see her again. Mirrors were on all of the surrounding walls; an expensive oriental rug accented the plush, black leather sectional. To the left, there was a pole in the middle of a dance floor.

Everyone sat around drinking and getting high. Someone had bought enough weed, coke, and pills to make some small time hustler retire out of the game. The music was bumpin' and as I peeped the scene, I couldn't believe that Janaya hung out here. My dad would never believe it either. I laughed as I pictured Genise's face if she was ever to find out what her daughter was doing.

All of a sudden, the lights dimmed and "Da Stripper's Anthem" from Gangsta Boo started playing. I knew that Janaya wanted to borrow my CD, but I had no clue at the time that it would be to make a CD to shake her ass to.

I took a seat in a corner of the couch while Shawn went to get us some drinks. I decided to take it easy because I was the designated driver. He sat the drinks on the table as the music started. Janaya came out and began dancing when the rapping started. I couldn't believe that she was doing the damn thang! All the dudes around us were drooling. She did a split on the pole and started popping. A couple dudes ran up to her and put money in her g- string. She danced and winded around the pole and then it was Robin's turn. Robin came out and did her thing like a pro. The stud chick and some other dudes came and put money in her g-string. After they danced for a while, two other girls that I hadn't seen when Janaya and Robin were getting dressed came out and danced.

After they danced, I thought that it would be a serious orgy up in there. I saw Robin take two dudes to a room to get her freak on. Janaya and the other girls soon followed taking random people back to private rooms.

"You havin' fun?' Shawn asked.

"Yeah, I'm cool," I answered. I couldn't believe that Janaya was a 'ho' like that, but to each his own. I just wanted to know if the money that she made at the end of the night was worth it.

It was about two in the morning and we were still chillin'. Shawn and I vibed all night. He grabbed my hand and asked me to follow him. I got up and we walked off down a separate hallway away from the party.

"This your house?" I asked.

"Yeah, me and my cousin live here. To tell you the truth, I'm 'bout to get my own spot. You like it though?"

"Hell, yeah!" I said as he pulled out a key to unlock the room door. I had only had one drink so I was cool, but I knew what was up. I was feelin' Shawn, so I was down.

"Come on in," he said inviting me into his bedroom. Shawn closed the door behind us. He pulled out a remote and turned on some music. It was quiet on his end of the house. The house was just that big. I wondered what he did to live this large, but I knew. It wasn't like I hadn't been with a hustler before. But I could tell he was big time.

He dimmed the lights and walked over to me. Shawn grabbed my hands and led me over to the high four-poster bed that was decorated with maroon silk sheets, a silk spread to match, and gold accent pillows.

I sat back on the bed as Shawn lit a blunt. I hadn't had any weed in a while and I gave in. It wouldn't bother me if I just had one smoke. I would still be able to drive home. As we sat back on the bed getting high, I remembered how horny weed used to make me. Plus, I hadn't had any weed or sex since Mark and since Shawn was sexy as shit, he would be getting it tonight.

We finished the blunt and he sparked another one. He smoked that mostly by himself as we chilled. We knew that it was on, after that.

Shawn came over to me and started undressing me as he exhaled the last of the smoke into my mouth. I caught a contact and exhaled the rest of the smoke as he took off the last of my clothes. My DKNY sweat suit sat in a pile on the floor as I laid back in my matching red panties and bra. Shawn took a minute to admire my body and then stripped. When he got down to his boxers, I could see that he was standing at attention, ready for me.

Shawn did things to me that I had never had done. Granted, I had only been with two other men, but damn! Shawn had a stroke that had me climbing the walls. I couldn't get enough. He let his tongue travel all over my body and I let him take command. This man was a professional at what he did, so I let him do his thing.

"So Mia, when do I see you again?" he asked, as we lay there in our own sweat and juices when we had finished.

Shit, whenever you want, if you laying it down like that! "All you got to do is call me," I said.

"You not a freak like your sister, are you?"

"Hey, I didn't even know that she did all of this," I confessed. "How long you known her?"

"Oh, she's one of Big Deuce's girls," he said casually.

"Big Deuce?"

"Yeah, he's my cousin. We're related by blood, but we aren't the best of friends anymore. That's why I'm 'bout to dip out this crib. He's a pimp."

Damn, it all made sense. She wasn't doing this just for extra money. She was getting pimped.

"You a pimp too?"

"Naw, that ain't my thing. I been watchin' him get these girls that are younger and younger everyday. I can't watch that anymore. I do other things."

I heard what he was saying and I got the point that he didn't want to say too much more. Hell, he had said enough already.

We exchanged numbers and Shawn said that he would get up with me that weekend. He told me that he didn't want to make this a one night stand and that he had enjoyed spending time with me. It was crazy, because we had vibed that night and there was this immediate connection.

By the time I found Janaya, she was completely fucked up. She had sampled all of the drugs at the party, not to mention having more than a few drinks. I practically had to carry her out of there. I would have never guessed that she rolled like that. I hoped that while she was in the room with all of those men, she had used protection.

I got us home safely about four in the morning. We crept back into the house just as Janaya said we'd be able to. I was glad to shower and change.

Lying in the bed, I couldn't get Shawn out of my mind. It was a casual meeting and I was down with that. I knew that there was a chance that he wouldn't call me back, but I wasn't going to be mad if he did get back to me so we could get together again without all of the other people around.

Even though I had showered and changed, my body was still tingling from the sex we had. I wished that someone had told me that somebody could put it on you like that. As I turned over on the bed, thinking about what I was going to do later that day, Janaya came into my room.

Closing the door behind her, she came and sat on the edge of my bed looking like hell. Her hair was everywhere and her makeup was smudged all over her face like she had been crying.

"Mia?"

"Yeah?"

"Thanks for coming with me tonight," she said softly.

"Sure. I couldn't let you go out like that alone. Look, it's late and I'm going to get some sleep." I turned back over and buried myself under the covers.

I felt her get up off my bed and heard her as she opened the door.

"Mia?" she said as she stood in the doorway.

I didn't answer. I only waited for her response.

"I just wanted you to know that I'm not a 'ho'." Janaya closed the door to my room. I heard her loud and clear, but after what I had seen and found out about Janaya tonight, I wasn't so sure.

Chapter 16

I woke up that morning feeling ready for a new start. 2003 would hopefully be a new beginning for me. In the fall it would be my senior year in high school, but, ,most importantly, my mother was coming home tomorrow. It was appropriate that she would be home on the first day of the New Year.

As I stretched, the quiet of the house fell on my ears. I thought over all of the events of this past year. So much had changed. But then and again, change was the story of my life. Nothing was ever really stable.

I was happy to have my dad back in my life, but I missed my mother. It was a fact that I tried to deny, but I yearned for a better relationship with her. I had faith that things would be different this time around. She was stable on her medication for her mental illness and she, most importantly, was clean. I was very proud of her.

My dad said that he thought that it would be best if I finished up school by staying with him. My first impulse was to disagree. I wanted to be with my mom, but I knew that it was for the best. Besides, I was not ready to move again. The next time I moved it would be when I moved out on own, at eighteen years old.

I wrote my mom a letter and told her that although she was coming home, I would rather finish school and stay with my dad. To my surprise, she agreed. She thought that it would be best. Our mother-daughter relationship was completely different now. She told me that we had to prepare for our roles to change. I would no longer relate to her as child to an adult. From this point on, it was young adult to adult. It was a lot to look forward to, and both of us were excited. She was happy that I was doing well in school and living with my dad. She felt that she had disrupted things enough and she just wanted the best for me.

Things with my dad on the other hand were not as great a picture as I had painted in my mind. Don't get me wrong, it was no problem living in this outrageous house, having my own car, and plenty of freedom. Daddy worked crazy hours and he was hardly ever home. When he wasn't working, he was at some social event. Not to mention that in the next election, he would put in his bid to run for Fulton County Judge. So things were always hectic around the house - when he was actually at home.

Then there was Genise. I knew that she hated me from the second my dad told her about me. She had always known about his life with my mom, and me but for some reason, I guess she hoped that since we were out of sight, we were out of mind.

I know that she was beyond pissed when I moved in, and for the past couple months, I tried to play it cool. I only spoke to her when necessary and she returned the favor. Having a car and a license gave me the freedom not to have to hang around the house with her drunken ass.

And when I say drunk, I mean drunk. This chick got tore up on the weekends when Daddy was out late working. Hell, what am I saying? There really didn't need to be a celebration for her to hit the bottle. Janaya said that she had been drinking a lot more since I was here. And the news of my mother coming out of the halfway house encouraged her to grip the vodka a little tighter. Maybe she was jealous or insecure about the relationship that my parents had. After all, he had completely paid off the house that we lived in and he continued to pay for the rest of the bills and utilities while my mom was away.

I heard them fussing one day about it and he flat out told her that he would continue to pay for things as long as I was a minor under his care. Maybe he was still stuck on the fact that he had walked out on us and that was his way of making things halfway right. Plus, it would have been really trifling' if he lived like he did with all of that money and he left his oldest daughter broke and without. I couldn't be mad at him. I had friends who had baby daddies that didn't give a shit about them or their child and would rather party first and give the leftovers to them later.

Genise was really not a problem for me, but somewhere deep down, I wished that things could have been better between us. Janaya was cool, but it tripped me out how this chick partied. On the outside, she appeared to be this straight-A student who was involved in every activity and club that her mother could make her be part of, but inside, she was insecure and looking for love in the wrong places. I realized that Genise was more into making things appear to be great instead of actually living that way. I wondered if she knew that her beloved daughter was out there 'hoeing' like she was. It was probably hard to see through her drunken stupor.

Janaya was out there. She sampled any drug and any man that came her way. I asked her once how many men she had been with. "At one time or just period?" was her answer. I couldn't believe that this pretty little girl had turned out like that. Big Deuce was pimpin' her, but not in the conventional way. He had her dancing at private parties, which was the new thing. She never even really brought home any money, just a hundred here and there and maybe some new clothes and jewelry. I didn't understand because those were things that her parents could buy her.

The courts in Georgia had been really tough on pimping. There were serious pimping rings that stretched from Atlanta to Detroit and there were girls running away from home looking to hook up with these pimps.

Janaya had this fascination with living in "the streets". I couldn't figure out what it was about. My life had never been all that bad. I had seen people living worse. My mom and me were kind of ghetto fabulous. Like I said, my dad was still paying for things and now I knew how that left my mother money to be able to afford things for me that other kids in my hood couldn't have; new tennis shoes, expensive purses, nice clothes. I knew that Janaya hung around me trying to absorb some street smarts. She had never seen some of the things that I had and for some reason she wanted to be exposed to all of that. She was the suburban girl that had watched one too many fake rappers on the music videos.

After I met Shawn, we started to spend more time together. He was only nineteen years old. Although Shawn's work was questionable, he was a good person. He was the type of guy who opened doors for me and encouraged me to do well in school. He wanted to see my report cards and wanted me to do things in life after I finished school. He said that I had too much potential and he didn't want to see me ruin myself like the girls that his cousin was pimping.

Shawn made it known to me that the things he did were not always legal and he didn't want me to get caught up with what he was doing. But it didn't stop me from hanging with him. We went out and had a lot of fun together. Unlike Mark, Shawn always had me home on time to get up for school.

With us, it wasn't about the sex, which was surprising because we did it the first night we met. Shawn said that after getting to know me he wanted much more for me than I had even wanted for myself at that moment. Don't get me wrong, the sex was good, but we could chill and not even think about that. We talked and sometimes the conversation made me feel closer to him than anything intimate or sexual could.

The only problem was that Big Deuce was mad that he couldn't get me as one of his hoes. After he had seen me at the party, he wanted to put me on. Especially because Janaya was my sister. He figured he could sell us together. I straight up told him that I wasn't interested.

I came past one day to visit Shawn and I heard the two of them arguing about it. Deuce said that if he caught me around again, he was making sure that I would be one of his 'hoes'. Shawn told him that he wasn't having it and that his girl was not a 'ho'. His girl. He had called me his girl. I couldn't help feeling good about that along with the fact that he was fighting for me.

"Look, Mia, I don't think that it's good idea that you come by here anymore," Shawn told me. "From now on, we can meet somewhere or I come and get you. You understand?"

"Yeah," I said.

Soon after, Shawn got his own place and we chilled there. He still had business with Deuce, but he was trying to get away from working with him for other reasons that he would not mention. Now we had the peace of mind that we could be alone at his crib without Deuce trying to get at me.

For New Years' Eve, I was going to see the Peach Drop with Mookie and Marissa. Shawn was supposed to join us, but called me and said that there would be a change in plans. That he had to go to Miami for some business.

"Damn," I said, while I was picking out an outfit for the evening. "I was looking forward to you meeting my cousin."

"I know, Mimi, but I'll meet him when I get back."

"Okay. How long will you be gone?"

"I don't know, but I'll call you and let you know."

"Just make sure that you call me to say 'Happy New Year' at midnight. I was looking forward to all of us being together."

"I know, Mimi. Hey, one more thing," he said. I could hear that he was already in the car on his ride down to Miami.

"Anything."

"Get a piece of paper. I want to give you some info. I need you to keep this private though."

"Sure. One sec, let me grab a pen. Okay," I said, as I got ready to write the info, "What is it?"

He gave me a series of numbers and an address.

"What is this?"

"Don't worry about it. You'll know when you need it. I trust you. And Mia?"

"Yeah?"

"I want you to know that I've never trusted any other chick but you. No one. Not even my own mama. She asks me for money all the time, but that's all it's about with her. I don't really have any other family but Deuce and you see how that's working right now, so all I got is you."

I listened as he spoke and I couldn't believe that after a few months, we had become so tight that he would trust me like he did. But I trusted him too. As a matter of fact, I knew that I loved Shawn. I thought that I had loved before, but this was the real thing.

"Mia?"

"Yeah?"

"I love you. Just know that. Now I gotta go. I'll call you at midnight."

"I love you too, Shawn." He had read my mind.

"Have fun tonight. Later."

I hung up, not really wanting to. I had just seen him last night and he hadn't said that he loved me to my face and now he chose to say it over the phone. I took the numbers that I had written down and put them in my jewelry box for safe keeping and locked it. From the sound of the conversation, Shawn was acting like he wasn't coming back. He was just tripping'. I couldn't wait until I saw him again so that I could hear him say that he loved me, face to face.

My dad and Genise got ready to go to the Governor's mansion for a New Year's fundraiser. Janaya was going to spend the night at a friend's house. I was going to spend the rest of the weekend at Aunt Lena's so that we could pick up my mom the next day. I was excited to see my mother again. When I walked downstairs, my dad and Genise were on their way out of the door in their black tie attire.

"Happy New Year, Mimi!" Daddy said, as he kissed me on the cheek.

"Happy New Year to you too, Daddy. Same to you, Genise. You two look great."

Genise and my dad looked at me curiously. I had never really paid her a complement.

"Thank you, Mia," she answered.

"You have fun and tell Lena and Mookie that I said have a great holiday."

Genise rolled her eyes at the mention of my aunt and cousin.

"Cliff, let's go or we'll be late," she said as she tugged on his arm.

"Bye, Daddy," I said as the two of them left.

I closed the door behind them and went to get ready. Janaya had already left for the evening with her friend Allison.

Before I left, I called Marissa and told her to catch the train and Mookie and I would meet her at the Indian Creek station. I made it to Aunt Lena's and, as usual, she was working, so I waited for Mookie to finish getting ready.

"So what's been up, cuz?"

"Nothing' much," I answered.

"Who's the lucky man?"

"What are you talking about?"

"The way you came in here all happy and shit, it could only be one thing," Mookie said. "A good brother can do that to you. I should know. I always have satisfied customers."

We both looked at each other and laughed. Mookie was a real freak and he wasn't quiet about it. I told him all about Shawn, minus that part about the sex on the first night.

"I'm happy that you finally got yourself someone worth your time and someone your own age. You and those older dudes really had to stop. They only wanted one thing."

"And I guess you know all about that too?"

"Me? I don't fuck wit' younger chicks like that! What I look like messin' wit' jail bait?"

Just then Marissa called and said that she was passing the Kensington train station. Mookie and I left to meet her. On the way there, we talked about my mom coming home. I told him how excited I was and how much I was looking forward to a new start in '03. He was too.

Apparently his music career looked promising. Troy had kept his promise and Mookie had been in the studio putting the finishing touches on his demo. Troy had also promised to help promote him as an artist and help him get put on a record label.

I was happy to see Marissa. We talked all of the time, but with school and living on the opposite side of town, we didn't really get to see each other much anymore.

When we got downtown to Five Points, it was crowded. Winter in Atlanta can be cold at times, but tonight it was just cool enough to wear a light jacket and a hat. People were standing around talking and celebrating as we waited for the New Year to come in. We went to get something to eat and window-shop in the closed stores along the mall at the Underground.

It was finally 11:55 pm and the countdown had begun. We got a great spot to look at the sparkling Peach as the music played signaling that it was almost time to start the final countdown. The Peach dropped slowly and the news crews could be seen covering the event. We all laughed and I hugged my cousin and then Marissa.

I pulled my cell phone out of my pocket and looked to see if I had any missed calls. I was really looking to see if Shawn had called any earlier to say he loved me again. He hadn't and so I put the phone back in my pocket, still clutching it, in case it vibrated. The final countdown began and everyone was screaming out as the Peach dropped, "5-4-3-2-1! Happy New Year!"

The Peach dropped and the '2003' sign lit up on top of it. We all laughed and cheered and hugged each other and wished a happy new year to others around us. We stuck around for a minute to allow some of the crowd to leave after the celebration. Marissa was going to spend the night with us at Aunt Lena's and then I would take her home when we went to get my mom.

By the time we got on the train, it was after 12:30 am.

No call from Shawn yet.

I didn't even get mad. As a matter of fact, I was nervous. I caught myself glancing at my phone every few seconds waiting for it to ring. I sat back as the train whizzed by each stop. I knew that something was wrong.

Chapter 17

THE PHONE RANG FOR THE FIFTH TIME AND THE VOICE MAIL CAME ON:
"Leave a message."

Short and to the point. I had listened to Shawn's voice repeat the message over and over for the last four hours.

I was nervous. Why would he call and tell me he loved me and give me some important info like he did? Maybe he already knew that something was going to happen to him.

I threw my cell phone down on the bed and tried to get some sleep. My mom would be home in the next few hours. Aunt Lena would pick her up on her way home from work in the morning. I couldn't sleep and being worried about Shawn was killing me.

I was going to wake Marissa up, but I had talked her head off about my worries all night. She finally fell asleep on me a couple hours ago. I got up to go to the kitchen. It was five in the morning and I was wide-awake. Obviously Mookie wasn't asleep either as I found him fixing a bowl of cereal.

"What are you doing up?" he asked, pouring the Fruit Loops.

"Can't sleep. Pour some for me too."

He handed me a bowl and a spoon and poured the cereal. We sat down and ate in silence.

"What's up, Mimi? Ole Boy ain't call back yet?"

"No, and I only get his voice mail when I call. I'm just worried."

"Give him a chance. He'll call you. Don't think the worst. I'm sure he can handle himself."

"That's the problem. I'm not sure exactly what he was going to Miami to do, so I don't know what to think."

"Mimi, you know what type of cat he is and you know what type of work he's doing. Just chill."

I wanted to get my mind off of things so I changed the subject. "So what's your first single going to be?"

Mookie laughed. "I don't know about that yet, but I'm almost finished the demo. I'm going to get it in the right hands and get myself out there. I feel good about it," he said, as he finished his last spoonful of cereal.

"Cool, I got to hear you sometime. All this time and I never actually heard you rap."

"Damn, you haven't heard me yet! Well, you will in due time. So, you excited that Aunt Tricie's coming home?" he asked before drinking the milk from the bowl.

"I am. I'm glad that she did what she had to do to get herself together. But I'm still going to stay at my dad's until I get out on my own. I only got a year of school left anyway. What you going to do after you graduate in May?"

"The music of course. Troy's got some connects in the industry."

"I guess Aunt Lena still doesn't know you're dealing with him."

"Mimi, I got to do my thing. I know what he does, but he's a good dude. He doesn't bring all that around me so I'm not trippin'."

I jumped when I heard my cell phone ringing. I looked at the clock and it was quarter to six in the morning. Mookie and I had been talking in the kitchen for an hour.

"You better get that. It could be the call you were waiting for," Mookie said, as he went back to his room.

I ran back to my room, leaping over Marissa like an Olympic track star while she slept on the floor, and dove onto my bed. I grabbed the phone and flipped it open.

"Hello?" I said, out of breath.

"Mimi, what you doing out of breath so early in the morning?" Shawn joked.

"Shawn, where the hell you been?" I couldn't help but yell at him. The sound of his voice brought me relief that he was okay.

"I told you I had work to do. Why you been blowin' up my phone? Twenty missed calls makes you look like a stalker," he said, as he laughed.

"How could you laugh at me? I was so worried about you!" I confessed.

"Aww, ain't she cute!"

I couldn't help but smile. "You on your way back?"

"I am. I just wanted you to know that things were aight. I know your mom's coming home today and you're going to do the family thing. Call me later?"

"Yeah," I said, as I closed my flip phone.

"I told you he would call," Marissa said, as she rolled over.

"Yeah, you did."

"He all right?"

"Yeah."

"Good, now go the hell to sleep."

I had to laugh at my friend. Shawn was okay. Now the only thing I had left to do was face my mother tomorrow. And that was a piece of cake.

Aunt Lena told us that my mom wanted to go straight home so Marissa and I drove back to meet them at our house. I dropped Marissa off at her home. She wished me good luck and we promised to get together in a few weeks.

I drove down the street and parked in front of my house. It felt good to be home, despite all of the memories. It was the New Year and I was determined to let those things go so that I could have a better relationship with my mom.

I put my key in the door and before I could open it, the door pulled open from the other side. As I came in, my mother pulled me into her arms.

"Mimi! I missed you so much!"

I gave in to her embrace and we stood there for almost an eternity. I couldn't believe that she was home. I looked up and saw that she was crying. She looked good. She had gained some weight in all the right places. When she was on the drugs, she had lost too much weight.

"You look good, Mama!"

We sat down on the couch and she told Aunt Lena and me about her journey. She was six months clean and she said that she was not turning back. She was taking her medication for her bipolar condition regularly and she understood the importance of staying on the medication as well as the side effects of coming off improperly.

She laughed and smiled and sat before us, a new woman. Aunt Lena and I told her how proud we were of her.

"I see you got a car!"

"Something like that. Daddy took me to get my license and he gave me that car to drive."

"Guess you're living it up over there, huh?" she joked.

"It's cool."

"Don't get me wrong, I'm happy for you, Mimi. I'm glad that you and your dad are back together again. You needed that."

We sat back on the couch in silence, absorbing the moment.

"I just want to tell you two how sorry I am for everything."

"Tricie, you don't have to apologize," Aunt Lena said.

"No, Lena," Mama said holding her hand up, "I do have to apologize. I was selfish and I made some mistakes that could have cost me my family. I wasn't thinking clearly at the time and I wasn't doing right. But I promise myself and my family that I will, from now on. I have an interview for a job in two days. I have to get back on my feet."

"Well sis, you know I got your back emotionally and financially. Just let me know what you need."

"Me too, Mama. I'm here for you, too."

"Thanks ladies! Now, I'm hungry. Why don't we go and get something to eat?"

"Sounds good to me," Aunt Lena said.

We got up to go out and eat. I had to admit, my mom was glowing. I don't ever remember seeing her look so good in all my life. It was like the weight of the world was lifted off her shoulders and she was ready to conquer anything.

Shawn was safe and my Mama was a new woman; I couldn't have asked for a better start to my New Year.

Chapter 18

Summer 2003

IT WAS THE SUMMER BEFORE MY SENIOR YEAR IN HIGH SCHOOL. I TURNED seventeen in the spring and my cousin Mookie had graduated from high school. My aunt was so proud of him. I had never seen her as happy as she was the day that he walked across the stage.

Afterwards, he got a job at the post office at night and went to school part-time at the community college. The rest of the time, he spent at the studio. My aunt still didn't know that he was in contact with Troy. I didn't feel good about his association with Troy for some reason, but my cousin was his own man.

My mom was doing well. She had a job as a receptionist and she was working full time. I was proud of her recovery process. She decided that it was best that she take things one day at a time. I thought that was the best advice for her. She limited her activities to her Narcotics Anonymous meetings, working, and visiting with Aunt Lena and me.

I was working at Cobb Galleria. I needed to be able to get out of the house and do something productive for the summer. Plus, I wanted to make my own money.

My relationship with my dad was great. We went out to lunch and spent a lot of time together by ourselves when he was home. Janaya on the other hand was getting more and more 'out there' everyday. I was confused as to how my dad and Genise didn't notice. It couldn't have been because Janaya was smart enough to get over on them. They were just blind. She had way too much freedom for her age.

That was the other reason that I went out and got a job; I wanted to be as far away from her shit as possible.

Shawn and I were also doing well. Yeah, he was still doing his thing, hustling', but I didn't mind. He was encouraging to me and for the first time in life, I thought about going to college and making something of myself. I even brought him by to meet my dad. They hit it off immediately and I knew why. Their personalities were a lot alike. They both treated me like a princess. We told my dad that he worked at his cousin's company and kind of left it at that. I was glad that my dad didn't ask too much more.

It was a Friday night and I had just put in a long day at work. I was tired and looking forward to going home. As I usually did, I called Shawn up to talk to him while I was on the way to my car.

It was after eleven when I got home and I was happy to be there. I hung up with Shawn after we agreed to meet when I got off from work the next day. He wanted to take me shopping.

When I came in, my dad and Genise were leaving to catch a late movie. I was glad that they were leaving and that I wouldn't have to watch Genise get toasted another weekend. Janaya, of course, took that opportunity to leave out to go and do her thing. She had been dancing at more and more parties. At the rate that she was going, her shit would be sagging by the time she was twenty. It was to the point that she didn't even ask me to go out with her anymore. I made it clear that I wanted no part of what she was doing.

She told my dad and Genise that her friend was picking her up and that she would be spending the weekend out. They agreed, as usual, because as far as they knew, Janaya was a good little girl.

I heard her yell, "I'm outta here, Mimi!" as she walked past my bedroom door. The front door was shut and I was all-alone in the house, happy for the silence. I made some popcorn and called up Marissa. We talked for a few about what was going on in the 'hood. We were going out next weekend get outfits for the Birthday Bash - the annual concert given by one of the local radio stations.

The next thing I knew, I had fallen asleep and woke up to my cell phone ringing. I missed the call and stretched as I rubbed my eyes and looked at the clock. Four in the morning. The phone line that Janaya and I shared started ringing.

"Hello?" I said, picking up on the first ring. All I heard was crying. My heart started racing.

"Janaya? Is it you?"

"Mimi, please come and get me! Please," she yelled between cries.

"Where the hell are you?"

"Downtown, near the bus station. Hurry!"

I got dressed and left the house. I raced downtown as fast as I could. I circled the block twice and the third time, as I turned the corner, I saw Janaya come out from behind the bus station building. She saw the car and ran over.

She was crying, her makeup was smeared, her clothes ripped, and her hair was all over her head. She looked as if someone had seriously fucked her up.

"Please, just take me home, Mia. I don't want to talk about it," she said, cutting me off before I could ask any questions.

We went back home and went to our separate rooms. I sat up and watched television knowing that she would come in and want to talk. She showered for what seemed like hours. Afterwards, she came into my room and sat down on the edge of my bed, wrapped in a plush terrycloth robe.

"I told Big Deuce that I wanted out and he made it clear that it wasn't happening. He smacked me around a few times and when I tried to fight back, he ripped my clothes and almost raped me. So when I got the chance, I left the party that I was working and called you."

She paused for a minute and waited for my response. I just sat quietly and waited for her to finish.

"I don't want to do this anymore. I know you don't believe me, but I don't. I know that I'm nothing like those girls who do that."

"So are you finished for good? Can you really get away from this for real?"

"I will. I don't know what I would do if my parents found out. I have to start doing right," she said. "I just wanted you to know that I want to give it all up."

I reached over and gave her a hug. Her body shook as she cried. It was crazy because Janaya and I were a lot alike. We shared the same father and both our mothers struggled with addiction. It just confused me how she could turn to look for love in prostituting. I told her that I would be there for her; after all, I knew what it felt like to look for love.

She didn't know that I could understand the feeling of abandonment and wanting to belong, more than she knew.

Chapter 19

I CAME HOME FROM WORK THE FOLLOWING SATURDAY TO SEE THAT WE
had visitors. I pulled up and saw a Cadillac in the driveway and
wondered who was here.

As I walked into the house, I heard laughing in the family room.
I was hoping that I wouldn't have to stick around and entertain
because I was going to hit the club with Carmen. She was a friend
that I met at work and found out that we had a lot in common.
We were hanging out a lot lately.

Carmen Vega was a year older than I was and she lived on her
own. She worked at our workplace as her second job to help make
ends meet. Her family was as crazy as mine was and she said that
when she turned eighteen, she moved out with her older sister to
get an apartment. Her older sister had recently moved out with
her boyfriend and Carmen wanted to keep the apartment, so she
worked two jobs to pay the bills until she could find a roommate.

I walked into the family room and the sight that I saw made
my blood boil. Everyone stopped laughing and turned, all eyes on
me.

"Mimi, I knew you would be surprised," Daddy said.

Surprised was not the word. Pissed was more like it.

I turned around to walk out before I said something that I
would regret.

"Mimi, you're not going to come on over and give your
grandmother a hug?" the woman that I had once considered to be
my grandmother, asked.

That was it. That comment took me there. I looked around the
room and saw my grandmother, my Uncle Jeff, my Aunt Delinda,

and my Aunt Camille. After all this time here they were in the family room laughing, talking, and having drinks with my Dad and Genise like it was all-good.

"No, thanks," I replied. I know they didn't think that I was going to be happy to see them.

"Well, I know it's been a while Mimi, but the least you could do is come on over and sit with us a while," my grandmother said. She sat there, all decked out in a designer outfit and plenty of jewelry.

"My name is Mia," I said. "And let's not talk about the least that someone can do."

I turned to leave.

"Mimi, come on. I thought it would be a good idea for you all to get reacquainted," my dad said.

"Sorry Daddy. It wasn't one of your best ideas. Excuse me. I have some things to do this afternoon." My uncle put down his drink and rubbed his forehead; Aunt Delinda just stared, tears welling up; Aunt Camille rolled her eyes; my grandmother chose to make a comment.

"Well, I think that's just plain rude, Mia. We all flew here to come and see you and you are making plans? I assume that you can rearrange your schedule?"

I decided to take the time to get some things off my chest. I had about ten years of anger bottled up. "You know what? I didn't ask any of you to come here. My dad did. Now he and I have worked some things out and I have forgiven him. But how dare you come in here like I owe you something after all this time! No one has called me in the past few years, let alone even sent me a letter to get in contact with me. You all chose to take sides after my parents split up and left me sitting high and dry!

"Grandma, how can you sit there on your high horse and tell me about the least that I could do? Where have you been? In case you all haven't noticed, I'm seventeen years old. It's been like ten years since I've talked to any of you. What happened to all of the phone calls and holidays, huh?" By this time I was yelling and I felt the hot tears welling up, but I didn't want to show that I was truly hurt.

"I went through some real shit," I continued. "It was bad enough that my dad left, but my mother had issues too. Maybe you never really did like her and you pretended to be cool with her because she was with my dad. But some family you were! When they split up, you stopped coming around after a while. I didn't want all the bullshit gifts you all gave me when I came by for the holidays. I wanted to spend time with you all like we did when my parents were together. I wanted to feel like I was still part of the family. But what did you all do? You put yourselves into my parents' relationship, chose sides and left me assed out. Well, I hope you don't think that you can come in here now and that I'm gonna be happy about it. I've done fine without you all this time. I definitely don't need you now! Daddy, I'm leaving for the night. I can't stay here. This is too much!"

They all looked at me, my Aunt Delinda with tears in her eyes. I left and went to pack my clothes for the evening. I decided to call Carmen and ask her if I could stay the night since we were going to the club anyway.

Carmen said it was cool. There was a knock at the door as I packed my toiletries. My dad opened the door and didn't wait for me to answer his knock. He and my Aunt Delinda stood in the doorway.

"Mimi, I'm sorry, baby," he said, as he grabbed me and gave me a hug. "I thought that it would be a good idea since you and I have built a relationship. I should have talked to you first."

"You should have, Daddy," I said, wiping the tears away.

"Mia," Aunt Delinda started. "I'm so sorry about all of this. I was young too. I was in high school and I never really realized what was going on during that time. When Cliff called and said that you and he were reunited, I wanted to be here so you and I could get acquainted again. I wanted to see you and I didn't think that maybe you would feel this way."

I looked at my aunt, who was strikingly beautiful. She looked like my dad, except that she was more brown-skinned and she kept her thick eyebrows arched. She was dressed really fly and I felt like she and I had a lot in common just from our brief encounter.

"It's okay," I told her. "I appreciate your apology. I just felt a little attacked in there. The way Grandma came off was completely out of line. I was a kid then and I was looking for you all to be adult in the situation and that didn't happen so I wrote everybody off."

"Here," she said. "I want to give you my number. I live in Cali and maybe we could get to know each other and you could come out there and visit one day. I'd love for us to become close. We're not that far apart in age, you know."

She wrote her info down and placed it on my dresser. "Call me when you're ready. I'll let the others know how you feel and tell them that you need some time." She smiled and walked out the door. I could appreciate that.

"Daddy, I'm going to spend the night at Carmen's. We're going to the club tonight and besides, I need to get my mind right after all of this."

"Sure, Mimi. I understand. I'm sorry I sprung it on you this way. You go and have fun. I'll see you in church tomorrow."

"Actually, Daddy, I have to work tomorrow, but I'll be home for dinner."

"Works for me, Pumpkin." He squeezed me more tightly and gave me a kiss on my forehead. I grabbed my overnight bag and left by the backdoor. The afternoon had been crazy. I was glad that I had got the chance to get all of that out of my system. There was a time when I would have been happy to have them come back in life. I couldn't believe that they came in with the attitude that they had. Maybe I could get to know Aunt Delinda again. She was only ten years older than me. And besides, she seemed like the only one with a level head and an ounce of regret.

By now, I couldn't really give a damn about the rest of them. It took them ten years to come back into my life. I could be happy that they came back around, but I figured I had gotten this far without them. Why would I need them now?

Chapter 20

"Tu abuelita really has some balls doesn't she?"

"Hell, yeah! But I don't know what my dad was thinking," I replied to Carmen.

We were getting dressed to go out. I was looking forward to having a fun night out to clear my head. Carmen and I always had fun. We had hit it off immediately when we met.

Carmen knew first hand what it was like to have a dysfunctional family. Hers would make a best-selling novel all on its own. She was a spicy Mexican sister; long black hair, medium height, and petite waist, round hips, big brown eyes, and attitude for days. She was the second oldest of six siblings. Her father was often abusive toward her mother and she decided that it was best to get out of the situation ASAP.

"Well, you know the offer still stands. You're welcome to move in with me if you need to, chica." Carmen brushed on the last stroke of lipstick.

"Thanks," I said. "I may just take you up on that soon enough. I'm ready. Let's go."

We went out to the club. Of course I used my fake ID. Carmen insisted that I get one since she was already eighteen, about to be nineteen. "I can't believe you don't have one already!" she said, when she found out that I didn't. I told her that I really didn't go to the clubs much.

"You live in Atlanta and you don't go to the club? Aye!..." she exclaimed and proceeded to ramble on in Spanish. She took me to a flea market off Buford Highway and once I got the ID, we had been going out ever since.

We had a great time at the club. Carmen and I danced with everybody, including ourselves. You know how girls do it, in a small circle dancing with one another, telling the ugly guys to beat it.

It was definitely a girl's night out. We turned off the cell phones. I told Shawn and she told her man, Manny that it was all about us tonight.

We left the club about three in the morning. After stopping at the Waffle House, we went back to her crib to chill out.

I showered and changed as Carmen was jonesin' on the phone with Manny. I knew she couldn't survive an entire night without talking to him.

I picked up the phone to call Shawn. The phone said that I had fifteen missed calls and six messages. What the hell?

The phone rang in my hand.

"Hello?"

"Hey, Mimi? How was your night out?"

"Cool. We had fun." It was Shawn. "Baby, you didn't have to call me so many times. I told you I was going out with Carmen."

"Well, maybe you should check your messages, 'cause it wasn't me," he said. Okay. Now I was nervous.

"Hey, I'll call you back in a few."

"Yeah, let me know if you need anything," Shawn said before he hung up.

I skipped checking the call log and pressed the button for my voicemail.

You have six messages...Beep... "Mia, where are you!"

I paused. It was my Aunt Lena sounding frantic. My heart was racing.

"Mia, you have to call me back! It's Mookie! Oh God!..." her voice trailed off between sobs.

I pressed the speed dial number for my aunt. The phone rang one too many times. I hung up and called her cell phone.

"Mia?" It was my mom answering the phone. I could hear my aunt crying in the background.

"Mama! What's wrong?"

"It's Mookie, baby. Are you alone?"

"No! Mama, please! What's wrong?"

"Baby, who is with you?"

By now Carmen had come into the living room and was asking me what was wrong.

"Carmen. I'm with my friend, Carmen. Mama, what is it?" I was scared to know the answer.

"Can she drive you down to Grady?... Mookie's been shot baby!" All of a sudden, my mother wasn't calm anymore and I became unraveled at the sound of her crying.

Did she just say that my cousin just got shot? I asked her to repeat herself.

"Mimi, pass the phone to your friend."

By that time, I barely remembered passing the phone. The room was spinning and my feet gave way under me. Carmen grabbed the phone as she helped me to sit on the couch while she took some information from my mother.

It was hard to breathe. I couldn't loose my cousin. I had to get there as soon as I could. I wasn't going to believe this until I saw it for myself.

Carmen rushed me downtown to Grady Hospital. Everything was happening so fast. I hadn't stopped crying since we left the apartment.

The elevator door opened to the waiting room and I saw my mother sitting with her arm around my aunt. Aunt Lena sat with her head in her hands as my mother read from the Bible.

"Oh my God! Where's Mookie?" I said running over to them.

"It's going to be okay, baby. It's going to be fine," my mother said standing to hug me. She turned to look at Carmen. "Thanks for getting her here safely."

"No problem," Carmen said sitting down next to me.

Aunt Lena was too distraught, so my mother filled us in on how my cousin was doing so far. It seemed that Mookie was out at the studio when some boys ran up on everybody in there and started shooting. Two of the other people in the studio were killed and there were three others here at the hospital. We were just waiting for him to come out of surgery.

We sat around for at least another two hours. Carmen called my dad and let him know where I was then led us in prayer. As we said "Amen", a young male doctor came out to the waiting room. The other two families there, along with us, turned attention to him, each hoping that the information he brought was of our family member.

"Ms. Reed for Michael Reed?"

"That's us!" Aunt Lena replied, as we all jumped up.

"Things went well in surgery. The bullet just missed a main artery in his leg, so he was very lucky. He'll most likely have a limp, but otherwise, he's in good condition. He's resting now, but you can see him. Follow me."

We all breathed a sigh of relief that he would be okay. Carmen gave us all hugs and left. When we went into the room, I almost wanted to faint as I saw my cousin hooked up to all the machines. He looked peaceful as he slept on the crisp white sheets.

Each of us pulled up a chair around his bed and thanked the Lord that he was okay. A policeman came in and gave us his card and asked that Mookie call when he woke up so that they could get a statement from him.

"I just don't see what he was doing there," Aunt Lena said as she kissed his hand.

Both she and my mother looked at me knowing that my cousin and I kept tabs on each other.

"Aunt Lena, you know that Mookie wants to rap. He's been working on his demo," I said quietly.

"Why? He's too smart for all of that street thug shit! What the hell does he want to be a rapper for?"

I just shrugged because I knew that this whole situation had something to do with him hanging around Troy.

"Don't bother Mimi, Mama," Mookie said, coming to in a groggy tone.

"Just relax baby! Don't try to talk," Aunt Lena said. My mom moved closer to his bedside with a cup of water to wet his mouth.

"No, Mama. I'm fine, really," he said taking the water, sipping slowly.

Just as he came to, the officer returned to the room.

"Mr. Reed, I would like to get your statement while it's still fresh in your mind. We would like to find the men who did this."

"Sure," Mookie said pushing the button to make the bed sit up.

"We were in the studio," he started, "and as one of my boys laid his last verse, I heard a commotion outside. We heard the shots and all of us tried to break out. As I ran, I got caught in the leg. I got to my car okay which was parked around the back of the building. I got down in the driver seat to wait for the shooting to stop. About a minute later, I heard someone get in a car and ride off. I went back into the studio and saw that Ray and Deebo were shot in the head, point-blank, T was shot in the chest, Jay was shot in the arm, and John- John was just grazed on the temple. We called the ambulance and here we are."

The officer took notes as Mookie talked. "You are very lucky, Mr. Reed."

"Blessed. He's blessed," Aunt Lena interrupted.

"Uh, yes, he is," the officer responded. "Mr. Terrell Johnson just died in surgery. Mr. Jason Bell and Mr. John Grooms are going to be released from the hospital this morning. Mr. Grooms did shoot and kill one of the suspects. We have reason to believe that the boys who shot you all were trying to get back at a Mr. Troy Jones. Do you know anything about this?"

Mookie bit his lip trying to search for a response as I saw recognition come to Aunt Lena's and my mom's faces.

"Troy! No, not Troy! My son would not be around him!" Aunt Lena said in denial as she shook her head in disagreement. Mookie just sat quietly.

"Tell him, Mookie!" Aunt Lena screamed.

"I'm sorry ma'am. Do you also know Mr. Jones?"

"Mr. Jones was a friend of my son's father," she said to the officer. "Mookie, answer him," she said turning her back to my cousin.

"Yes, I know Troy," he said keeping his eye on Aunt Lena.

"What the hell do you mean you know Troy?" Aunt Lena asked.

Mookie told her how he and Troy had met at the Underground. He told them how he had been hanging around with him and how he had been laying down some tracks at Troy's studio.

"Thanks, Mr. Reed. We will be in touch," the officer said before he left.

"How could you Mookie? How could you hang out with a thug like Troy? I thought I raised you better than that?" Aunt Lena said angrily.

"Lena, this is not the time," Mama said.

"Oh hell, yeah it is! This boy has been hanging with people like Troy and could have been killed. I want answers now!"

"Look, Mama, I met Troy and he was cool. He has been good to me and is supportive in my rap thing. You never want to really know what I'm doing. All you want to know is that I'm not hanging in the streets like my dad!"

"Boy, watch your mouth! You're lucky you're in that bed or I would tear into your ass!"

"Why, Mama? Because I mentioned my father? Hell, you never do! You act like he was a horrible piece of shit! Troy tells me good stories about him and you when you were happy. Now all you do is work all the time. You never go out or do anything unless it's with Auntie Tricie. Troy said that you used to be so much fun. He said that you really loved my dad and that the two of you were inseparable and that my dad was going to get out of the game because I was going to be born."

Aunt Lena was in tears and I could tell that what Mookie said had taken her back to a time that was long forgotten. My mom just rubbed her back as Aunt Lena sat crying.

"Your dad was a good man, Mookie. He just made bad decisions," my mama answered. "Troy was right. Your parents were like Frick and Frack. He was so happy that you were going to be born. He would have been proud of you."

"Mama, it's okay to talk about him. You never show me any pictures or anything. Troy did. And I appreciate what he did for us."

Aunt Lena looked up at him curiously.

"I know about him giving you my dad's stash," Mookie said.

"Did he tell you how much it was?" she asked.

"No, he said that you and I should talk about that."

"Patrice and Troy are right. Your dad was a good man, but he was stuck in the streets. Crack had just hit and there was a lot of money to make. And I can't deny that I enjoyed how he spoiled me with that money. It just hurt so much when he died. I always knew that it could happen because of him hustlin.' But I never really said anything about it until I got pregnant. He said that he would get out the game and that he had some cash stashed. I had no idea how much.

"When he died, I went home with Patrice and Cliff to stay for a while since I had a new baby. Troy came by to tell me that he had something for me. He had taken the money and started a couple bank accounts and CDs that he put money into for us. He said that we would never have to want for anything. He bought us the house we live in and made sure we were taken care of. I eventually asked him to leave us alone because seeing him reminded me of your father and I couldn't take that. So he left us alone and left me with all of the bank info. I've never touched the money all of this time and I just let the bank statements roll in. I thought maybe this year I would finally invest some, but it's been hard for me to touch the money.

"I'm sorry, baby. I just thought that it was better that we not talk about him so that you wouldn't miss what you never had."

"Mama, I've missed him my entire life. I wanted to know who he was. If I am anything like him. I'm a part of him too."

Aunt Lena leaned over and hugged Mookie. "I love you so much. You are all that I have."

My mom and I gave her a hug. They both left Mookie and me in the room alone while they went to go get drinks and snacks for us from the vending machine. I walked over to Mookie's bedside and gave him a playful punch in the arm.

"You scared the shit out of us!"

"Yeah, I know. My bad."

"So, you eventually gonna tell Auntie that Troy is financially helping you with your rap career too?"

"Naw. I think she knows enough. I'll leave things where they are. I ain't tellin' her that Troy's laundering his money through the studio. You think I'm stupid? Hell, what she'd do to me if she realized that I knew about Troy still hustlin' would be worse that getting shot! What she doesn't ask, I won't tell!"

Chapter 21

2004

"Baby, I'm out the game."

I looked at Shawn out of the corner of my eye as he maneuvered the car off the highway. I didn't say anything as we waited at the light before we made the turn into the parking lot at Perimeter Mall.

"Did you hear me, Mimi?"

"Yeah, I heard you. When did you make this decision?"

"Damn! You act like you ain't happy to hear what I said," Shawn exclaimed as he turned off the ignition.

"No, don't get me wrong. It's just such a surprise. I'm happy you are," I said grabbing his arm, trying to calm him as we walked toward the mall entrance.

We went straight to the food court to grab something to eat before shopping. We both chose the food we wanted and found an empty table.

"So, what do you think?" he asked, resuming the conversation.

"I think it's great," I answered taking a bite of my food. "I'm just a little concerned for your safety."

Shawn put his burger down and took my hand. "I'll be fine. I'm tying up loose ends now. Look, I'm getting older and I don't want to keep doing this forever. You're eighteen and I'll be twenty-one at the end of the year. Now that you've graduated from high school it's time that you really started living your own life. I just

want that to include me. And if I'm going to be around, that
means I need to get legit."

Shawn leaned across the table and kissed me on the cheek. I
couldn't help but smile. He was a good man. He never cheated
and he was always up front and honest with me. For the first time
in my life I had a relationship with someone that made me feel
secure. It was a feeling that I never really had with my own parents.
I know that being eighteen didn't entitle me to having a whole lot
of experience with serious relationships, but I knew a good man
when I saw one. And I saw one in Shawn.

Mookie had recovered from his gunshot wound. He still had a
slight limp in his walk. He let the music thing go for a while and
continued to work at the post office and take some night classes at
Georgia Perimeter. Aunt Lena finally took some time off from work
to spend some personal time with Mookie. She decided to share
her memories of Rob, Mookie's father, with him. He said for the
first time in life, he felt that he was complete.

My mom was doing very well. She kept her promise to stay
clean. She was working full time and even thinking of going back
to school. She said that she had never really wanted to go to school
to study law and that she had sacrificed her needs for my dad. She
had really wanted to be an interior decorator but thought that
going into law would make her more money. I was proud of her
and the fact that our relationship was improving.

I had graduated from high school in the spring. I was looking
forward to starting school at Clark Atlanta University in the fall to
get my degree in Biology. I was finally going to move out of my
dad's house and move in with Carmen so that I could live on my
own. My dad was against it and wanted me to stay with him and
just concentrate on school, but I wanted my independence. My
dad agreed to pay my rent and utilities in exchange for my not
working during the school year and concentrating on school and
getting good grades. I could work during the summer. I thought
that it was a good deal.

When I came home from spending the weekend with my mother, I walked in to find Genise pacing the floor frantically.

"Mia, have you seen Janaya?"

"No, I haven't heard from her this weekend. Why?"

"I thought that she was spending the weekend with her friend Amy. I just spoke with Amy's mother and Janaya hasn't been there all weekend!" Genise said, clutching the phone so tightly that her hands were turning red.

Shit! Janaya was still out trickin'. She had promised me that she was going to stop. Since I had graduated, I spent less time at my dad's and so I hadn't seen her or spoken with her in almost a week.

"I can try her cell," I offered.

"I have, several times," Genise said, breaking down in tears just as my dad breezed through the door.

"Genise, what's going on?"

"Oh God!" she said crying and throwing herself onto my dad's chest.

"Mia, what's going on?" Daddy said, looking at me curiously while he tried to comfort Genise.

"She said that Janaya is missing. She was supposed to stay at Amy's and Amy's mother says that she hasn't been there all weekend."

"What!" he yelled. "Genise, give me the phone. We have to call the police."

I was worried about her. Truly worried. Knowing what she was into, I just hoped that she was safe.

Chapter 22

THE DETECTIVE ARRIVED SHORTLY AFTER WE CALLED. IT WAS AMAZING how quickly the police responded in the nice neighborhoods. He immediately pulled out a pen and a notepad to begin gathering information.

"District Attorney Lawson, Mrs. Lawson, do you know of anything else that could help us out in this situation? I think I've covered all of the bases, but if you know anything else that may help it would be great," the detective said, after asking all of his routine questions.

"No, I think we've told you everything," Genise said. "What else could there be?"

"Well, sometimes when teens disappear, they go off with friends that their parents don't know about."

"What are you trying to imply, Detective?" Genise snapped, uncrossing her arms.

"Nothing Ma'am. Just trying to help."

"Well, I think you've helped enough! Now, please leave!" she screamed, pointing toward the door.

"Excuse my wife, Detective. This is all just so sudden," my dad said trying to smooth things over.

"No problem," he replied. "May I ask you if you know about any of your sister's other friends?" the detective questioned as he turned to me.

I paused for a minute, wondering how to work the fact that Janaya was prostituting, into the conversation. I knew that I needed to tell, but right now the news would be devastating.

"Well, she has been going out to these parties."

"What!" both my dad and Genise exclaimed.

"Parties?" the detective asked.

"Yeah, with a guy named Big Deuce. She met this girl named Robin, or something like that, and she got her into dancing at these parties."

"You mean, she's a prostitute?" Genise screamed.

"Thanks," the detective said, writing down the information I gave him. "That will help us out a lot. Big Deuce leads a prostitution ring that spans from Georgia, Tennessee, Alabama, on up to Michigan. We'll be in touch," he said handing my dad his card. My dad walked him to the door and promised to call if there was any more information. The detective left us there wondering where Janaya could be and what would happen next.

"You ungrateful bitch!" Genise said as she lunged at me. The next thing I knew, we were on the floor, fighting. I felt bad about fighting this grown woman, but I wasn't about to let her get the best of me. I threw in a few quick punches before my dad could sprint across the floor and separate us.

"Ladies! What the hell is going on here?"

"Cliff, this ungrateful bitch has got to go! How dare you call my daughter a 'ho'! You've got room to talk with your heroin addicted, dick suckin' mama! Get the fuck out my house!"

I couldn't believe Genise had even let those words come from her mouth. The situation with Janaya being missing was bad enough, but she had lost her mind throwing my mom in the mix.

"Well, it looks like my mama ain't the only one that sucks dick! Maybe if you put the drinks down wit' your drunk ass you might have known that your daughter was sneakin' out the house sellin' her shit like she was. You know, you might have my daddy fooled wit' your uptight, stuck-up attitude, but I see you for who you really are! Don't think I don't know that you trapped my dad into getting you pregnant so he could pick you up and wipe your dusty, ghetto ass off and give you a better life, you gutter bitch!"

We lunged at each other again. All the rage that I felt was ready to come out and I was going to fuck Genise up some more if she wanted it.

My dad had to physically get between the two of us to stop the fighting.

"Genise! Get yourself together! I can't believe you! You're an adult, she's a child!"

"Yeah, well let me go so I can whip her ass like a grown woman!"

"Daddy, I'm outta here," I said as I picked up my purse and keys, brushing past him. "I don't have to take this shit from your wife. Oh yeah, and maybe you should check the stash that she keeps outside in the pool house. The bitch has enough liquor out there to start her own package store! Call me if you find Janaya."

I turned to walk out just as the phone rang. My dad pushed Genise back with him toward the phone, still shielding her so as not to allow for another fight. I noticed that her nose was bleeding and with her hair everywhere, she looked like the crazy bitch she was.

"Hello?... Janaya? Where are you?... We're on our way!"

Genise grabbed the phone and continued to talk to Janaya. My dad raced for his keys and threw open the front door.

"Mia, let's go! Call the detective and tell him that we are on our way to get Janaya now!"

Chapter 23

WE FOUND JANAYA STANDING ON A STREET CORNER NEAR A DIMLY LIT GAS station. She rushed to get into the car. When we saw her standing there, I felt sorry for her but at the same time I was angry that she had let that lifestyle pull her back in. The little bit of clothes that she had on was ripped and when she got into the car, the overhead light showed us that she had a black eye.

"Are you okay, sweetie?" my dad asked pulling Janaya into his arms.

"I think so," she said, as she began to cry again.

My dad gave her a once over as the detective pulled into the gas station parking lot accompanied by another police cruiser. It was a quiet area and there were few people outside at that time of night. A black sedan rolled past slowly and rounded the corner.

"Is everything okay?" the detective asked.

"Yeah, she's in one piece," my dad answered.

"Did you see anyone else in the area when you pulled up D.A. Lawson?"

"No, she was standing here alone," my dad said as he started the car.

"Janaya, is it possible that anyone has followed you here? How did you get here?" the detective questioned.

"No, I don't think anyone followed me. I ran out the house where I was and I don't think that anyone even knows I'm gone yet," she answered.

"Detective, do you think that we can get her to the hospital to get checked out first before you get her statement? I would also like to call her mother and tell her that she is safe."

"Uh, sure. Why don't you all follow me?" The detective and the officer both got back into their cars and we followed them to the highway. I looked in the rearview mirror and saw that the black sedan I just saw driving down the street had turned the corner along with us. When we turned to get on the highway, the sedan made a right and turned back in the direction we had come from. Maybe they were on to Janaya and figured out that she had escaped.

Genise was on her way to meet us at the hospital. Janaya explained to the detective about how the night went down. She went to Gainesville with at least three other girls. Her friend Robin, aka Candy, found out that Deuce planned on taking them to Michigan to do some work there. She wasn't having it, and she told him that this would be her last party. She had no way of getting home because Deuce had driven all of the girls to the house in Gainesville in one of his limos. Deuce wasn't happy that Robin didn't agree with the situation and slapped her around a bit. That's when Robin reached into her purse and pulled a gun on him. Deuce laughed and told Robin to remove herself from the group because he wasn't going to have her cause any trouble for them. Everybody knew what the meant. One of his boys, Shorty, was asked to "take care of her".

Janaya said that she heard Robin go outside with Shorty, who was the loose cannon of Deuce's crew. A few seconds later, they heard Robin scream. Then there were two gunshots.   H i s tactic had worked. The rest of the girls were scared out of their wits. They decided to go through with the party so that they would not meet their end as Robin had. Deuce told them that Robin had to be dealt with because he wasn't going to stand for anyone messing with his money.

Janaya went through with the party and waited until everyone was completely intoxicated so that she could make her getaway.

She went to change her clothes for the next set and locked herself in the bathroom, pretending to get sick. She climbed out of the bathroom window and called home on her cell phone after she left the house.

She hid in an alley for a while to wait out her escape, hoping that no one had immediately come looking for her. Luckily, we were able to get to her before anyone found out she was gone. This was all a bit too much for us to handle. I was torn between wanting to protect Janaya and being pissed at her for putting herself in the position that she had. I was happy that she was safe though and said a quick prayer for her as I left the hospital. I told her that I would be in touch with her later.

My dad let me drive his car home because I wanted to leave before Genise got there. I called Carmen and told her that I would be moving in sooner than I thought because of the altercation between Genise and me.

I went home to pack some of my things. I was going to stay at her crib until I could finish moving all of my things out. It was 12:30 in the morning and I decided to call Shawn to see if I could stop by before going to Carmen's.

I got to Shawn's, and walked through the door to find some bags sitting at the front door.

"Where are you going?" I asked, with attitude. I already had a fucked up night. Shawn leaving was the last thing that I needed.

"Look, I got one last thing to take care of. I'll be gone for a week," he said, without looking at me.

"Oh, yeah?"

"Yeah. You got a problem with it?"

"Hell, yeah, I do! What happened to gettin' out the game?" I asked.

"I am, Mimi! But you don't just stop cold turkey. Come on, now."

"So you lied?"

"No, I didn't lie. I am gettin' out! I just need to take care of one last thing."

That wasn't exactly what I wanted to hear tonight.

"So, what are you going to do?" I asked with my arms crossed.

"Now you know that I can't tell you all that. I'll be back. Hey, what happened to you?" he asked, after brushing my hair off my neck and seeing the scratches from the fight.

"You know what? Fuck this. I gotta go," I said, throwing my hands up.

"Oh, so now you all big and bad, huh? Sit down, Mia!"

"Hell, no! I'm out. I can't believe you lied to me. I thought you were leaving all that alone and now you say you got one more thing to do? I'm out," I said sucking my teeth and grabbing my purse and keys.

"So, it's like that? I don't remember you ever trippin' before when I made trips and came back with a grip of cash. You ain't had no problem spendin' did you? I told you the truth. This is my last time. I can make a clean break after this," he said grabbing my arm.

"Get off me, Shawn."

"Mia, stop playin'!"

"I'm so serious," I said twisting my arm away. No matter how mad I got, I knew that it wasn't going to change his mind about leaving.

"Mia, I know you're mad, but I'll call you when I get back."

"Don't bother!" I yelled, as I walked out of the apartment and slammed the door behind me.

Chapter 24

IN THE TWO WEEKS THAT SHAWN HAD BEEN GONE, I MUST HAVE LOST MY mind. He hadn't called and he was gone longer than the week that he promised. That's why when I saw Mark, I agreed to go out and chill with him.

My dad took Genise and Janaya out of town on vacation after what had happened. Janaya had been beaten pretty badly and raped. He felt that it was the perfect time to get them out of town while the police investigated what had happened. He wanted me to go too, but I decided that it was best that I keep my distance from Genise. It was best for everyone.

Living with Carmen was good so far. We got along well. She was hooked on her boyfriend, Manny. Hell, they were hooked on each other. He spent the night over a lot and they could often be heard getting it on in her bedroom. For the most part I didn't mind. Manny was respectful of the house and he was a real cool person.

Seeing Mark was a pleasant surprise. I was at McDonald's after coming from my Aunt Lena's. On the way out of the restaurant, I heard someone call my name. I turned only to see Mark getting out of his car.

Damn! He still looked good. Actually, he looked better than he used to. He was clean-shaven and dressed in some fly, hip-hop gear.

"Mia?"

"Hey!" I said, trying not to sound too excited. He walked over and gave me a bear hug and picked me up off of the ground.

"What's up with you?"

"Not much," I replied.

"Yeah, well you look good," he said as he grabbed my hand and twirled me around. "You always had curves in all the right places, Lil' Mama."

I blushed and remembered why I found Mark so sexy.

"Yeah, well I'm all grown up now," I said.

"Is that right?" he asked, licking his lips with a sexy grin on his face.

He gave me his number and told me to call him so we could get together that night.

I went back to the crib to change. That's when the guilt hit me. I was going on a date with another dude behind Shawn's back. I picked up the phone to call Shawn and got his voicemail again. What was I talking about? Shawn went behind my back and went back on his word to do 'one last thing' that had taken him away from me for longer than the week that he promised. And the nerve of him not to call me at all!

Before I knew it, it was seven o'clock. Mark said that he would pick me up at 7:30. Carmen was staying the weekend with Manny so I wouldn't have to hear her tell me that I was wrong to go out with him. I picked up my cell to call Shawn again. If he picked up, I promised myself that I wouldn't go out with Mark.

The phone went straight to voicemail right as I heard the car horn beep outside. Hell, I wasn't going to sleep with Mark. We were just two friends going out to the club to chill. I wasn't hurting anyone I reasoned with myself.

I took one last look at my cell, shut it off, and walked out the door. Shawn wasn't the only one who could shut his phone off when he was busy.

I had to admit that I reminisced when I got in the car with Mark. He was still sexy as ever. We actually enjoyed ourselves at the club that night. Since we were good friends with one of the club's owners we got into the VIP area. We ate and had a few drinks. Okay, I had more than a few drinks.

I was feeling myself because I was looking good in my heels, a pair of skintight jeans and a sheer top, with a matching tam, that I wore cocked to the side that completed the outfit. I knew I had the entire club on my tip.

Mark was checking me out the entire night. I had already told him that I had a man and that we were in a good relationship.

"So why you out wit' me?"

"I just figured that I would spend some time out with a friend," I answered.

We danced and I had a couple more drinks. He grinded on me every dance and after a while I spent more time pushing him off of me than I did dancing. I knew that he was getting hot and that it was time to go home. At about two a.m., when the club started to play the same songs over again, I told him that it was time for me to get out of there. The truth was, that the guilt of being out with him and enjoying myself, was killing me.

Mark was starting to get a little aggressive and it came back to me that our whole relationship was about the sex. Mark was a nympho and that obviously hadn't changed. I was ready to go home, alone.

I stumbled out to the car, the result of one too many Long Island iced teas. Mark just laughed at me and my drunk ass. I must have passed out in the car, because I didn't remember most of the ride home, only to wake up a couple blocks from my apartment.

"So, can I come in?" he asked.

"For what?"

"You know, maybe we can rekindle old times. Your man don't have to know."

"No thanks, Mark. I had a good time, though," I said, trying to turn him down nicely.

He sucked his teeth as his phone rang. That gave us a welcomed interruption.

"Yeah man, I'm about to drop her off right now. I'll hit you back in a few." He hung up the phone and took another look at me as if he was giving me another opportunity to change my mind. I didn't.

"Are you going to be all right going home alone? I could stay with you until your roommate gets there."

"I'll be fine Mark. You just wanna fuck anyway," I said, starting to slur my words.

He laughed at me again. I was getting tired of his snickering. Mark made the turn into my apartment complex. Two right turns and a left around the circle. He pulled up and parked in front of building 2510.

"Girl, you pissy drunk! Can you make it up the steps?"

"I'm aight! I been way mo' more drunk than this!"

I wasn't lying. I had gotten fucked up way worse than this before. I was still coherent enough to push Mark's hand off of my thigh as it crept up my leg.

"Oh, so it's like that, Lil' Mama?"

"Hell, yeah! I'm out." Truth was I could have used a little help getting out of the car. As the cool evening air hit me, I felt a second wind. Hopefully it would be enough to get to me to my apartment.

I stumbled out of the car. Mark laughed again.

"F- Fuck you Mark!" I stuttered as I slammed the passenger door to his black on black Benz CLK 500.

"Whatever. Later Mia," he said, as he drove off.

I was glad that he was gone. I was going to go in the house and call Shawn again, or wait until I heard from him—whatever it was going to take to get my evening with Mark off my conscience. I felt bad for going out with Mark. Shawn was a good man to me and I shouldn't have done it.

As I walked to the door, I remember thinking that it was awfully quiet out for an early Saturday morning. The people in the building next door were usually outside drinking beers and playing music to usher in the weekend.

I tripped again and decided that the high heels had to come off. Fumbling through my purse, I pulled out my keys. I reached my front door, high heels in hand, and never was I so happy that I lived on the bottom floor. It took me a second to get the key in the keyhole. My vision was a bit doubled and I made a mental note to lay off the Long Island iced tea the next time I went out.

The lock clicked and I was home, sweet home. Breathing a sigh of relief, all I could think of was getting in the bed and sleeping off the intoxication.

I didn't even bother to turn on any lights, not wanting to bother with anything that would make my head pound worse.

I wondered briefly where Carmen was and then I remembered that she was out with Manny for the weekend. Hopefully Shawn would come home and he and I could chill for the rest of the weekend in my spot, now that I had a spot of my own.

As I entered my bedroom, I let the heels and purse land where they may. The street lamp from outside cast an eerie shadow in the room.

The next thing I remember was an arm coming from behind, grabbing me around my throat. It squeezed relentlessly as I clawed at it, trying to be released.

I was picked up off of my feet and thrown to the bed.

What the fuck was happening?

"What the hell do you want?" I screamed.

The answer was a back handed slap to the left cheek. I rolled off the bed and scrambled across the room searching for my heels so I could clock this mutherfucka in the eye or something!

He pounced on me as I hit the floor. All I could see was a figure in all black; black gloves, black mask, black hoodie, black sweat pants, black tennis shoes.

I wished for a second that I had asked Mark to come in. But here I was, all alone being attacked. I wondered if this is how it happened when you saw stuff like this on the news. But I wasn't going to sit here and let this dude kick my ass in my own home.

We struggled on the floor for what seemed like hours. He was obviously stronger than me, but I wasn't about to lie down and die. Not tonight.

I surprised myself that I gave up such a fight considering how drunk I was. I guess my adrenaline was pumping something fierce. He finally punched me hard enough that it stunned me for a sec.

As I lay there, I felt cloth being inserted into my mouth and knew that he was gagging me. Shit! Had I even screamed this whole time? Did my neighbor next door, Ms. Lee, hear the commotion?

He grabbed me again and threw me on the bed. He tied my hands and legs to the bedposts. He straddled me on the bed and all I could do was say a silent prayer. Prayer was the only way that I would make it out of this alive.

I couldn't figure out who would want to hurt me. I wondered if he was going to rob me too. Or maybe he already had. I had no idea who this man was or what he would want with me.

I saw him pull something out of his pocket. He unwrapped a condom, slid it on. He had already ripped my shirt off and he proceeded to rip off my pants. The fight in me was dying. A sharp pain consumed my body as he rammed himself into me. Again and again, he roughly plunged in and out of me. A small cry escaped my lips. I knew that no one heard. He just kept going, as I lay there unable to defend myself. The only thing that I could do as the pain burned from my vagina was to transport myself to some far-off place. The places that I watched on the Travel Channel flashed through my mind. White sand beaches; azure, blue waters.

Just as I was on the beach, eating a vanilla ice cream cone, he stopped. I lay there and waited for what he would do next. I wanted to know who this man was and what would possess him to violate me like he did. He laughed and smacked me again. My body ached all over and my womanly area throbbed from the beating I took. All I could think of was if I would ever be able to have children. I was too young for my life to end like this. I tried not to show any fear, a skill that I learned on the streets. People like him fed off of your fears. All I wanted was for this to be over. I prayed that someone would come to my rescue.

I was going in and out of consciousness and I could hear someone frantically yelling my name. I kept hoping that it was Ms. Lee. There was a banging at the front door that stunned my attacker. Maybe someone had heard all of the commotion.

He quickly dismounted me and pulled up his pants. He got close to me in my face and I could smell his sweat mixed with my scent on him. I prayed that he was leaving.

I saw a familiar bop in his step, as he turned to walk toward the bedroom window. Where had I seen that before?

"Bitch, you lucky I don't have the chance to kill you! I came to bring you a message. Big Deuce say he ain't finished wit you yet! You took away one of his best 'hoes' and Deuce don't play about his money! We'll be back for you. Believe that 'ho'!"

I would have never thought that everything would come to this point.

Right when I placed a face with the name and the bop in the step, I blacked out after his black, gloved, fist came at my face.

Chapter 25

"MIA! MIA!" I FAINTLY HEARD MY MOM CALLING MY NAME. WHERE WAS I? I was too tired to open my eyes and the sharp pains in my body begged me not to move.

"Just sit still, baby. You'll be okay." Soothing hands rubbed my forehead and I heard a faint beeping sound before I drifted off to sleep again.

"What's up, Mimi?"

As I came to, I saw Shawn standing over me. When I opened my mouth to speak, I found that it was too dry and instead of words coming out, a cough came through that sounded as if I had been smoking for years.

"Here," he said, putting the cup of ice chips up to my mouth. "The nurse said to suck on these if your mouth is dry."

He smiled gently and I almost forgot that I had been mad at him. As I focused more, I saw the crisp, white, hospital sheets. The television played a repeat episode of The Jamie Foxx Show, one of my favorites.

"How long have I been here?"

"Three days," he answered.

"Wow, what hap-," I started to ask. Then it all came rushing back to me. I wanted to jump up and put on my clothes and find the bastard that did this to me. But I was in too much pain.

"Don't worry about it. I took care of everything," Shawn said, looking at me gravely.

"What do you mean, you took care of everything?"

"Hey, Mimi, you're up!" My mom rushed through the door, interrupting our conversation.

"Yeah, I'm glad you're here," I said, as she came to the bed and hugged me gently.

"Well, where else would I be? And your boyfriend, Shawn, has been keeping me company," she said, winking at him.

"Oh, really?" I asked, chuckling.

"Why didn't you tell me that he was so nice, Mimi? I like him. I think you've met your future husband!" she teased.

"Umm, maybe I'll let you two have a little time together!" Shawn said, trying to escape the conversation. "I'll go and call everybody and tell them that you are okay."

We both laughed knowing that he just wanted to get away from two women who were talking potential weddings.

"What's the last thing you remember?" she asked me.

"I don't know. It's all a blur. How did I get here? Who found me?"

"One of your neighbors heard all of the commotion and called the police when she saw a man running from your apartment."

So it was Ms. Lee. She had heard me, I thought to myself.

"Where's Carmen?"

"She had to go to work. She comes everyday after she gets off, though. She should be here soon."

I didn't want to tell my mother that I now remembered vividly what had happened. I wasn't in the mood to talk about it. Most of all I wanted to know what Shawn knew so that I could find out what he had done to "take care of things."

I was released from the hospital after three more days of observation. The nurses gave me some information about rape survivor groups. I had to come to terms with the fact that not only had I been beaten, but I had also been raped.

I wanted to go back to the apartment that I shared with Carmen, but Shawn thought it was best that I stay with him, so he could watch over me. Besides, the lease was up at the end of the month and Carmen had already found us a new place to live. She decided to stay out the rest of the lease at Manny's crib. She didn't think that it was safe for either of us to be there anymore.

My dad thought that I should go and stay at his house, but I told him that with my arm broken, I couldn't fight his wife fairly. Aunt Lena and my mom both wanted me to come and stay with them, but I preferred to stay the week with Shawn until Carmen and I signed the new lease.

Fortunately, I had escaped the beating with more emotional scars than physical ones. I had scratches and bruises and a broken arm, but my body would heal.

Shawn finished preparing dinner for us. He was no gourmet cook and so dinner was a box of Kraft mac and cheese and beef hotdogs. He brought it over to the table and we sat across from each other in silence. So far, I hadn't asked him anything about his comment at the hospital, but it was time for me to know what he was talking about.

"I'll tell you what I did," he said, reading my mind before I could even speak my thoughts.

I just sat back and waited for him to unfold the story.

"First, I want to say that I know you went out that night with another dude, but that's cool. I excuse that, but don't let it ever happen again." *Damn! How did he know?*

"Anyway, when I went out of town, word came through the grapevine about what Deuce did to that girl in Gainesville. To have that girl killed like that for nothin' was uncalled for. Then I heard that he had your sister up there too and I thought that hit a little too close to home." Shawn stopped and took a bite of his food.

"I told you a long time ago that I was through fuckin' wit that dude. And the reason that I had to go out of town at the last minute was because of him. Long story short, I had to clear some things up wit' an old connect that we had so that I could make a clean break from the game. I didn't want to go, but I had to so that I could move on with my life. With *our* lives.

"Then I come home and you're not answering your phone so I just come over. Carmen tells me what happened and I figured out what was up after they had it on the news how your dad's place got fucked up by a robber and how your sister was beaten and raped too. I knew that it was no coincidence. Whoever had done this had done it to the both of you and it looked like they were going after your dad because he was going to press some serious charges against Deuce and his crew."

I just stared at him as he talked because up until this point, I had no clue that anything had happened at my dad's house. I was glad that they had been out of town or who knows what would have happened.

"Your sister is very fortunate to have gotten out of Deuce's circle of 'hoes' when she did. He was ready to make a run to Detroit and do some major pimpin' and she may have never been found again. That Negro had some major issues and I would have hated for your sister to continue to be involved in something like that. All I'll say is that Deuce was really pissed off that your sister, his major moneymaker, was off the block. He said that he was loosin' some real cheese and that he didn't give a damn who her daddy was; she wasn't going to get away from him that easily.

Your sister was a real live 'ho' and her behavior could have had more serious consequences for your family than what actually happened. I told you that he and I had been going through it. My cousin was the type that preferred people dead as opposed to alive and cheating him out of his money. You know he was just related by blood and nothing else. I couldn't stand him after a while. He had tried me one too many times and I know that he had it in for me, too. The greedy bastard!"

"What did you do?" He kept speaking of Deuce in the past tense and it was scaring me. I figured that I had asked a simple question.

"Let's just say that my cousin and Shorty won't be fuckin' wit' anybody anymore… *ever again*. And why don't we leave it at that?"

I looked at him strangely. I was right. It was Shorty that attacked me. I knew that I recognized that bop in his step. I remembered it clearly because when I first saw him at the party where I met Shawn, I thought to myself, 'this dude bops so hard when he walks, he looks like an asshole'. Shorty liked to call it his 'swagger'. It really just made him look like the jackass that he was.

"You didn't do anything crazy did you?"

"Mimi, I said leave it. Just know that I would do anything, and I mean *anything* to protect you. I promise you that." He got up from the table, put his plate in the sink, and walked off to the bedroom.

Chapter 26

CARMEN AND I MOVED INTO OUR NEW CRIB. MY DAD HELPED US GET some new furniture and the apartment was hot! I loved the freedom of living on my own. Independence was a beautiful thing.

When I thought about it, having that freedom wasn't a new thing for me. I had never really had any real restrictions in my home. My mom had been on drugs and so she wasn't able to care for me properly after a while. I had to learn to do for myself at an early age. And then living with Aunt Lena, she wasn't ever really there because she had thrown herself into work to make herself forget how lonely she was. When I lived with my dad, he just tried to pacify me because he felt guilty for leaving my mom and me. Yeah, the freedom wasn't new, but the feeling of having some independence was.

I was now an adult, legally, and now was the time that I needed to make some choices about what I was going to do with my life. And those choices were all mine to make.

Attending Clark Atlanta was great. I was doing well in school and I loved my major. For once in my life, things seemed stable.

It was the last of the nice days of the fall and Carmen and I decided to invite our families and friends to a cookout at the park.

We got a pavilion at the park and set up all of the food. Manny began throwing down on the grill. I was putting out the last of the food when my mom, my aunt, and my cousin walked up.

I was so happy to see them here. I thought about how far we had come. My aunt finally decided to take some time off from work and travel. Come to find out, she had almost a million dollars in the bank that she had invested and saved over the years. She never really had to work all of this time, but she did, to escape the life that she had once known. Now she saw the importance of enjoying life and continuing to live, despite the death of a loved one. She and my mother would be taking a Caribbean cruise in the next month.

Mookie was still working at the post office and taking night courses in college. He was writing music and still wanted to get into the studio. He and my aunt had talked about buying him his own studio equipment and he studied media in school until then. He still never told her everything about Troy still hustling', but my aunt was smart and we knew that she already knew about it without us telling her.

My mom had done the best of all. She was going to start online classes for interior design in the spring semester. She sold our house and moved in with my aunt under the condition that the only way that one of them would move was if one of them finally got a good man. We knew that she would be there for a while. Neither she nor Aunt Lena were looking, they were enjoying their lives right now. My aunt was enjoying her time relaxing and just living. My mother was enjoying her life, substance–free, and she was continuing to work on living life with her mental illness.

The two of us understood that our relationship was a work in progress. I loved my mother and I was her biggest cheerleader. I couldn't really explain to her how proud I was to see her well after all of the shit we had been through, but somehow I knew that she understood how I felt.

Carmen's family arrived next, then Shawn. We all sat down to eat as the kids went off to the playground. A mean game of spades had begun just as my dad arrived with Genise and Janaya. I hadn't expected Genise to come along. I hadn't seen her or Janaya since I moved out.

"Hey, Mimi. I hope you don't mind that I brought some guests?" my dad said.

I looked over at Genise and Janaya. "No, there's food for everyone," I said, giving my dad a hug and a head nod to Janaya.

"I haven't seen you in a while," Janaya said, hugging me.

"Yeah, it's been a minute."

"I just want you to know that I'm out of all of that stuff I was doing, for good. I'm going to finish my last years of school at a boarding school. I've got to get out of Atlanta and change my focus."

"Really?" I asked. It seemed a little drastic.

"Yeah. I need to get away. I need to be more responsible. I was ruining my life and the lives of others around me. I'm sorry that you got mixed up in all of this."

"Well, everything's okay now, isn't it?"

"It is. I just don't want all of this to get in the way of our relationship. I've never had any siblings and I would give anything for us to be able to start over again."

I looked at Janaya for a moment and saw the tears forming in her eyes. "Well, I have only one sister and I can't let her get away from me that easily now, can I?"

We reached out and embraced each other, letting go of all the tension that had been between us. My dad nodded in agreement. He and Janaya turned to go and get some food as I turned to walk back toward my guests.

"Wait, Mia," Genise called out. My dad and Janaya stopped in their tracks. I almost did not turn around, but my curiosity got the best of me.

"Look, I know that I was a mean and ornery bitch. But I have to admit that having you in the home reminded me that Cliff had a whole other life before Janaya and me. That was hard to deal with and I took out my insecurities about that on you. I want to be woman enough to apologize for the way that I treated you."

I was stunned. I had actually received an apology from Cruella after all this time. I just hoped that it was genuine.

"You don't have to forgive me now, but I hope that you will some day. After all, Janaya misses her big sister. I would like the two of you to have a relationship and I don't want you to stay away on account of me."

"Thanks, Genise. That means a lot to me. Hey, you all go and enjoy yourselves," I said. trying to take some of the awkwardness out of the situation. Genise nodded her head. I just hoped that she would get herself to the nearest rehab for her alcohol abuse. She and my dad held hands as they walked over to the pavilion. Janaya turned around and smiled at me before she followed them.

I returned to the pavilion to try and see when I could get in the next hand of spades. Someone had whipped out another deck of cards, so by this time there were two games going on.

I saw my dad walk over and give my mother a friendly hug and I watched as he introduced her to Genise. She and my mom shook hands. I was happy to see everyone who meant so much to me gathered here together.

It had been a hell of a year. I couldn't wait until the beginning of the New Year. I had some resolutions to make. But for now, I wanted to make sure that I enjoyed spending every minute of this cool autumn day with my family and friends. There was a time in my life when I had thought that this feeling of peace would never be possible. But here it was!

I went and made a plate and sat down at the table next to Shawn. One of Carmen's many cousins struck up a conversation while the card game was being played.

"Hey, man. Did you hear about that pimp they found dead?"

"What pimp?" Another one of Carmen's cousins asked.

"I think his name was Big Deuce. They found him and some other guy from his gang, dead. They said whoever did it must have really had it in for him, because it was hard to identify them. They had to use dental records and fingerprints to tell who they were. Anyway, this guy was a big pimp in the south and he was into some real bad shit."

"Hmm, well I say that it's good to get trash like that off these streets. No one deserves to die like that, but I say, let street justice prevail," said another man at the table.

I looked to Shawn, to somehow make sense of what I was hearing. He pulled me close to him in his arms and kissed me on the cheek.

"I love you, Mimi," he whispered in my ear. "And when I promised that I would do anything to protect you, I meant it."

Acknowledgments

I HAVE TO BREATHE A SIGH OF RELIEF BECAUSE I HAVE JUST MADE ONE OF MY dreams come true. I have written a book that will be published for others to read. A dream that had been in the back of my mind for years. Something that would not come true unless I put in the time and the effort to make it happen.

I have to give special thanks to my girls who read *Promises Made, Promises Kept* while it was in rough draft form. Thanks to Aliya, Diondra, and Lisa for taking the time out, to not only read my work, but also to be completely honest with me about making changes and talking to me about what they liked and disliked about the entire project. That feedback made my story a better one.

Thanks to my husband, Arvin, for encouraging me to get started with the whole concept of becoming a writer. To my son, Sterling, for just being you. My sister, Nicole, (I figured I'd give you a break and not use your nickname for all the world to know) for jumping in on the reading too. To Ganny and Papa for telling me, a long time ago, that I needed to do something constructive with my imagination and for instilling in me the love of reading.

I also want to thank all the people that inspire me everyday to write stories. As a social worker by trade, I see people on a daily basis who are not always at their best. Sometimes when I see them, they have hit rock bottom. I see a story in every person that I meet and I also see the potential for a positive outcome in people's lives, if they are willing to put in the time and the effort.

I've had a tumultuous year and I realize a couple of things now as 2006 comes to a close. The good comes with the bad and no matter what happens in life, you have choices and decisions that are yours to make. You only have yourself to blame if you choose not to make your dreams come true. Set some attainable goals and go forth to achieve them. Don't let others dictate to you what you are capable of.

And lastly, live life as if there is no tomorrow. There is someone who did not see the sun rise on the today you woke up to.

Mommy, I miss you more than I can put into words. There is a void left in my life now that cannot be filled, but I know that I must continue to live. Life is too precious not to push on.

I hope you all enjoyed my book. Please feel free to email me with you comments, feedback, encouragement, etc. at sterlingsmommy_1221@hotmail.com or at myspace.com/maraangel.

Peace and Many Blessings,
Tamara

Printed in the United States
84628LV00001B/412-504/A